TRICK PLAY

HESTON U
PREQUEL

HOTSHOTS

USA TODAY BESTSELLING AUTHOR
VERONICA EDEN

TRICK PLAY

IT WAS NEVER
'FAKE' FOR ME x

HESTON UNIVERSITY KNIGHTS
#22 ALEX KELLER

HESTON

U

HOCKEY

TEAM ROSTER

ALEX KELLER, #22, LEFT WING
THEO BOUCHER, #14, RIGHT WING
CORY PUTNAM, CAPTAIN, #17, CENTER
EASTON BLAKE, #24, CENTER
CAMERON REEVES, #33, GOALIE
SHAWN HIGGINS, #64, DEFENSEMAN
JAKE BRODY, #47, DEFENSEMAN
DANIEL HUTCHINSON, #16, LEFT WING
CALEB ADLER, #68, FORWARD

COACHES

HEAD COACH: DAVID LOMBARD
ASSISTANT COACH: COLE KINCAID
ASSISTANT COACH: STEVEN WAGNER
FORMER HEAD COACH: NEIL CANNON, RETIRED NHL PLAYER

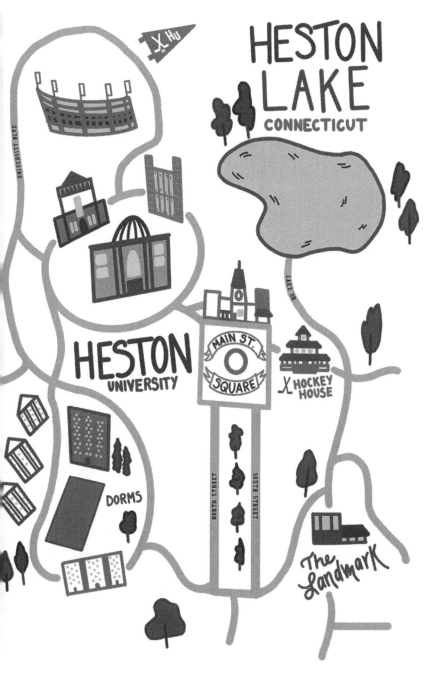

HESTON LAKE
CONNECTICUT

HESTON
UNIVERSITY

MAIN ST. SQUARE

HOCKEY HOUSE

UNIVERSITY BLVD

LAKE DR

NORTH STREET

SOTH STREET

DORMS

The Landmark

MAP KEY

HESTON CAMPUS
HESTON U ARENA
ACADEMIC LOOP
CAMPUS HOUSING

HESTON LAKE
MAIN STREET SQUARE, CLOCKTOWER BREW HOUSE
HESTON LAKE AND ICE SKATING RINK
THE LANDMARK BAR & GRILLE

PLAYLIST

Cool Kids — Echosmith
Fit In — Reagan Beem
Disaster — Conan Gray
Teenage Dream — Stephen Dawes
Beautiful — Bazzi, Camila Cabello
NIGHTS LIKE THESE — Benson Boone
Ballroom Extravaganza — DPR IAN
Fantasy — Bazzi
Paradise — Bazzi
Older — 5 Seconds of Summer, Sierra Deaton

HESTON U HOSTSHOTS SERIES

Heston U Hotshots is a series of interconnected college hockey sports romance standalones of Heston University's hockey players and their matches off the ice.

Perfect for fans of swoony and irresistible hockey players, feisty heroines, **spicy college sports romance** featuring tropes such as rival's sister, he falls first, grumpy/sunshine, fake dating, opposites attract, secret relationship, best friend's brother, and more!

These books can be enjoyed in any reading order as a standalone and feature glimpses of other characters/couples in the series.

HESTON U HOTSHOTS

Trick Play, #0 (*PREQUEL NOVELLA*)

Iced Out, #1

Switch Off, #2

Penalty Play, #3

Lucky Shot, #4

Line Shift, #5

RELATED HESTON LAKE STANDALONES

Matching All the Way

Scan the code to view the series:

ABOUT THE BOOK

Everyone in Heston Lake is obsessed with Heston U's hockey team except me. I'd rather do a live reading from the spiciest romance on my bookshelf *nude* than talk hockey.

I could ignore my college town transforming into a sports bar during hockey season, but there's no escaping the players fueling their obsession. My twin brother... and his best friend on the team.

#22. Alex Keller. Talented winger. The player every girl on campus dreams of.

And my fake boyfriend for the next two weeks.

His idea, *not mine.*

I doubt he knew I existed—until he stops the football team from teasing me. All it takes is a pet name and his strong arm around me. Playing along is my only option.

I'm ready to go back to my side of the divide between nerds like me and athletes like Alex, but he refuses. He's determined to protect me for real, even if our relationship is fake.

The only problem is…he's too good at pretending. Our act fools everyone—including me.

ONE
LAINEY

CAMPUS BUZZES nonstop about last night's hockey game. Everywhere I go, it's all I hear. The only thing people want to talk about is how great Theo and Alex's winning goals were.

Heston University—no, the entire town of Heston Lake itself—is obsessed with our ice hockey team. Whenever they play, my picturesque New England academic haven turns into the equivalent of a sports bar, like the one my dad owns in town.

I could ignore this transformation if it wasn't my twin brother and his best friend that everyone is so hung up on after a stellar season last year. They've garnered the town's obsession as the only two freshmen to earn starting positions and help take Heston all the way to the national championship.

My early acceptance to Heston University came first based on the merit of my good grades and hard work. Theo's came because Heston scouted him for the team, stealing my thunder and my chance to shine on my own instead of living in the shadow of my superstar athlete twin.

Guess which one of us Dad's more proud of? It's not my photo plastered all over his sports bar.

"For real, though," a girl gushes ahead of me on the snow-lined path to her friend. "It was insanely hot when Alex Keller took that final shot Theo Boucher passed to him. It does things to my body seeing them all aggressive on the ice, whipping those sticks around. Are you going to the party at the hockey house tomorrow night after the game?"

"Dibs on Theo," her friend replies in a saucy tone. "He can body check me right into his bed."

Oh god, *no*. Nope. I can't.

Pressing my lips together in a firm line, I scurry past them with my head down, automatically lifting a hand to adjust my glasses. Strands of long dark blonde hair fall forward to frame my face as a terrible vision of my life flashes before my eyes. I still have two more years of coping with the damn hockey season and suffering through people thirsting for my brother until I finish my degree.

The unpleasant mental image gives me the urge to drop what I'm doing, walk down to The Landmark, and hide behind Dad's bar snuggled up to Hammy. The white and tan eighty pound pitbull is the locals' favorite bar dog, but to me he's always been my emotional support and safety blanket after Mom left us when Theo and I were sophomores in high school.

The kicker? She dumped Dad for a hockey player in the AHL she'd been having an affair with.

Everyone in Heston Lake lives and breathes hockey.

Me? I hate hockey and I can't stand hockey players. As far as I'm concerned, the hockey season can't end soon enough.

I'm so lost in my agitated thoughts that I almost walk into another group of students crowding the wide path. Adjusting the bundle of books and flyers in my arms, I cast the fresh snow a dour look. If the early February storm hadn't blown through last night, I could've cut across the grass.

The three guys I almost ran into don't notice me, carrying on their conversation. "But did you see that freshman's crazy assist? That Blake kid's skating is unreal."

"He'll go pro. No doubt."

Great. More hockey.

"Wait, that's one of them isn't it? Blake!"

At the call of his name, a tall boy with messy brown hair and his friend pause nearby. They both have bulky dark blue gym bags slung over their shoulders with Heston U Hockey embroidered on them. If their warm up jackets weren't a beacon of who they are on campus, the recognizable bags would have given them away.

"You're Easton Blake, right?"

Easton shoots the trio of guys a roguish smile full of confidence and pride. His friend smacks his shoulder playfully with the back of his hand, grinning like an idiot. He adjusts his backwards baseball hat and steers Easton in the direction of the arena.

Uninterested, I seize the opportunity to slip by the group while they're distracted. I have so much to do for the event I'm planning to support the small family-owned bookstore I work at. There are only a few weeks left and my to-do list isn't getting shorter.

Hanging the flyers I'm balancing with the rest of my stuff is the top priority on the list today. I bite my lip. Before I can accomplish the task, I need to gather the courage to hang them. I'm much happier staying hidden between the shelves of the shop. I don't even handle the customers most days, leaving that to Mr. Derby and his daughter.

Putting myself out there and inviting people to see what I'm passionate about isn't something I'm used to.

I keep telling myself to suck it up, because this event I'm organizing is too important. Without the college and the town's help, the bookstore faces a corporate buyout from a chain brand. If that happens, it will undermine generations of one of Heston Lake's staples.

I won't let that happen. If I can get people to buy tickets to attend this charity dance, raising money won't be a problem. Derby Bookshop is a piece of this town's history that I care about.

It's the motivation I need to step out of my comfort zone. Everything about the event has been a lesson in challenging myself—talking to vendors, being in charge of the plans, petitioning the school to let me use a banquet hall on campus for the dance. All of it has stirred anxiety in the pit of my stomach throughout the process of preparing my Ballgowns for Books benefit.

Maybe Dad will let me hang some flyers around The Landmark. A lot of Heston students go there. It's a start. Small steps will get me up any hill that seems insurmountable.

I'm absorbed in a mental checklist as I navigate my way through campus. Keeping my head down is a mistake I don't realize until it's too late.

Everything clutched in my arms goes flying when I collide with a solid wall of muscle that towers over me. The colorful advertisements for the dance scatter the pavement along with my books and the journal with all of my important event planning notes. It falls open to the page with the final stages of organizing everything and I focus on it rather than the snickers sounding around the scene.

Large hands steady me. A thanks that will probably tangle on my tongue with the apology ready to follow dies when he speaks first.

"Finally ready to throw yourself at me, Lainey Brainy?"

Every muscle in my body freezes.

Not this again. Not today. Not *him*.

I squirm, intent on shoving myself back to get distance between us. Mike's fingers dig in. He chuckles, holding on a beat longer before releasing me. Being around him makes me frazzled. I swallow it back as he drags a hand through his hair, flashing his buddies observing the scene a smarmy grin.

The urge to run rises within me, but it would mean leaving my notebook behind. Weeks of hard work is in those pages.

Watching me with a smirk, Mike kneels at the same time as me, reaching for my notebook. I grip the end of it, tugging uselessly against the huge football player.

The only athletes on campus I can't stand more than

the hockey players are the football team. Namely, Mike River.

"Give it back," I say.

He pretends to consider my demand. "I don't think so. Say please."

I push my glasses up, ignoring the nervous thrum of my pulse. "Thank you for picking it up. I'll be taking it now."

He rips it from my grasp with an easy jerk. Flicking through the pages and glancing at the flyers covering the ground, he frowns. "When are you going to forget about these dusty old books? You're wasting your college life on this crap."

"That's Brainy for you," one of his friends says. "Books are all she's got going on in that big head."

Leave it to the jocks enrolled at Heston in the athletic track to not understand anything outside of their fans, their parties, and their sport. All things I don't care about.

Anyone who doesn't fit in with that lifestyle is labeled different. Strange. Despite college being a place where students explore our diverse interests and prepare for the next stage of adulthood, there are still too many people who put far too much stock in the importance of popularity like some social experiment gone wrong.

Rolling my lips between my teeth, I ignore Mike's question. Books are my escape from everything, but he doesn't deserve to know.

"Ballgowns for Books. Enjoy an evening of stepping into your favorite fairy tales to support a good cause," he reads, then snorts. "Oh, Brainy. No one's going to this dorky shitshow."

His dig hurts, but I smother the sting. My research suggested that a formal dance was the best way to attract attention. It wouldn't be my first choice, but it's the one I went with. It doesn't sit well with me that there's a possibility I'll fail to help the bookshop because I made a mistake.

I gather the flyers and my other books before shooting to my feet, aiming for a calm, direct tone when I hold my hand out. "I'll take my notebook, please."

His football buddies create a blockade around me, making escape impossible. I do everything in my power to avoid running into these guys, but today is all kinds of bad vibes.

"You're not trying to run away?" Mike cocks his head, rising to his full height. I purse my lips, caught out. "Nah, you're too smart for that, Brainy."

One of the guys coughs the word *nerd* into his fist. Original.

After a year and a half of sharing a campus with

them, I'm used to Mike and his friends making it their mission to taunt and humiliate me at every opportunity. If I stay quiet and out of the way, they usually get bored and move on.

Mike's cutting laugh makes me tighten my hold around the books I picked up. Any minute now. When they're still snickering, closing in on me instead of leaving me alone, I glance up and immediately regret it when he catches my eye. It's the same look he's given me since a freshman class we shared last year.

He's had it out for me because I turned him down when he asked me out to some frat party I had no interest in. Talk about tiny dick energy if his ego is that fragile because he's incapable of fathoming a world in which girls might not want the self-absorbed football player.

And what does he do for getting rejected? Goes out of his way to make my day difficult. What a winner. Definite boyfriend material qualities.

If only I had the courage to open my mouth and sling any of the well-thought-out comebacks I've formulated after our dreaded encounters, I'd put him in his place so fast. Instead, I stick with a demure mask of indifference in the hope my non-reaction to all of this will make him go away.

"I just want my notebook."

His eyes gleam and he holds it up out of my reach. "And I want you to get on your knees for me and—"

"Lainey. There you are, baby," another familiar voice interrupts, carrying an edge I've never heard. An arm slings over my shoulder and guides me against a warm, firm body, smoothly maneuvering himself between me and Mike. "You didn't answer my text. I wanted to see you before practice."

Confusion swirls over me. Why the hell is Alex Keller butting into my problem?

We have a strict unspoken policy of ignoring each other's existence that's worked since he became friends with my brother. What's he doing?

"Your text?" I stammer.

Mike's brows pinch and his eyes narrow as they cut back and forth between me, Alex, and the arm he's resting around my shoulders to tuck me into his side. He lowers my notebook, knuckles turning white.

"Baby? What, is she supposed to be with you or something?" The tone he uses shifts from a moment ago. He's cautious, as if Alex's intervention somehow gives me invisible protection against the immature games Mike enjoys playing with me. "Since when? Last I remember, you were at our party over the weekend with a hot sorority chick sucking on your neck before she took you upstairs for the main event."

I rein in a grimace. All jocks are shameless pigs only concerned with hooking up and their testosterone-fueled sports. Alex is no different. His sexcapades are the most commented on topic of gossip around campus when people aren't gushing about his skill playing hockey. He's known for scoring off the ice as much as he does on it.

Alex only hesitates for a beat before he doubles down. "It was just for show. You can thank my girl here. She's so shy, she insisted we keep things between us secret." He gives me a comforting squeeze. "See, babe? I told you I wanted to stop hiding that I'm crazy about you. I don't care about appearances."

I blink, darting a questioning stare at my brother's best friend. He doesn't have to lie or help me out. He's never gone out of his way to interact with me much before now, let alone bail me out of a sticky situation without any questions. I'd rather he didn't, considering I refuse to budge on my hockey players are the worst stance.

There's no way Mike and his crew will believe Heston U's ice hockey legend Alex Keller would be dating me.

Yet to my amazement, no one laughs like this is some elaborate joke I'm not in on.

"Hey, grab those?" Alex points to the few flyers I abandoned on the ground in my rush to escape Mike.

His tone remains light and his smile is easygoing, but I pick up on the subtle shift in his demeanor. It's an order, not a request.

Even amongst the jocks at Heston, there's a hierarchy and the hockey players are at the top.

The shock of this entire bizarre exchange fades for a moment as I take in Alex's handsome profile. Mike might be tall, but Alex has him beat by a few inches at six foot four. His light brown hair is trimmed on the sides and longer on top with thick waves that rustle in the cold winter breeze. More than his height, he has a captivating presence people swarm to thanks to his outgoing spirit. The charming smile he likes to throw around helps, too.

Once Mike's friends snap into action to gather my stuff, Alex motions to my notebook. "Is that hers, too? Thanks for helping my girl out, man."

Without asking, Alex takes it from Mike and offers it to me. Relief billows inside me once I have it. A muscle in Mike's cheek twitches, but he surrendered it without complaint.

The way he backs off so fast would be comical if it didn't annoy me that it's only because of Alex's presence rather than me handling this on my own.

The guy who called me a nerd awkwardly hands off the last of the flyers I dropped. With stilted movements, I accept them.

"There, that's better." Alex drops a kiss on top of my head, his warm hum causing a shot of heat through my stomach to chase away the biting chill in the air. His calloused fingertips graze my cheek, tucking my hair behind my ear. "I need to get to practice, or coach will lose his shit on me and make me skate suicide drills until my legs fall off. I need those for the game tomorrow to crush UConn."

I part my lips at the wink he offers, unsure what to say or do.

Mike saunters away backwards, casting one more grudging look my way that's a mix of longing and jealousy. "See you at the party tomorrow night after the game?"

Alex doesn't miss a beat this time, green eyes locked with mine as if he's seeing me for the first time. "We'll be there. Isn't that right, baby?"

Um, wrong. Very wrong. I won't be going anywhere near a party.

As soon as Alex walks away, this is all done and we'll pretend this never happened as far as I'm concerned.

TWO
ALEX

LIFE as one of Heston University's most talked about hockey players has its perks. I accepted Coach Lombard's personal recruitment invitation to play on his ice because he saw something in me that other top schools overlooked and it's the best decision I ever made. I saw Heston as the path that will get me where I want to be—playing in the NHL.

Since claiming the national title at Frozen Four last spring, my life has been great. I won't deny that I enjoy the fringe benefits. Everyone wants to say they know me, to befriend me, to climb in my bed. The icing on the cake is that my reputation and winning stats lay the groundwork for me, so it's go time as soon as I see the girls that shoot me sultry gazes and inviting smiles.

I'm here to work hard, but I know when to let loose

and enjoy myself. It's all about work-life balance. I would have liked to enjoy myself with the cute blonde heading my way giving me *the look* on my way to practice.

The interest evaporated the second I overheard Mike and his teammates harassing a girl. Through the small gap in their circle, I spotted Lainey Boucher bundled in her signature chunky knit sweater, eyes flashing behind her thick-framed glasses, and her mouth set in a trembling line I immediately despised.

No fucking way. The full body response iced me over from the inside out within seconds. No one else stepped in to stop them. No one was paying attention. Between one hard drum of my heart and the next, I pushed through the group to get to her with only one thought in mind: *I'll protect her.*

There's no chance I could've kept walking and ignored the situation.

Somehow I manage to keep my tone easygoing while my veins burn hot until Mike leaves believing she's mine.

Once he's gone, Lainey sags into my side with a sigh. The same protective urge I felt when I overheard those guys bothering her flares in my chest.

I didn't think before acting on instinct. Pretending to be her boyfriend wasn't the plan, it just came out naturally as the only way I could help my best friend's twin sister.

She only relaxes for a moment before she pulls away, putting a few careful paces between us. "Thank you, I guess. You didn't have to do that."

When she walks off, I follow. "Where are you going?" I don't get a response other than a jerky shrug. My brows pull together. "Class?"

Lainey won't look at me. I think she's pretending I don't exist or something. Maybe trying to ignore what went down. She's doing a shit job of it, almost peeking at me, then tearing her attention away and occupying herself with anything else. I cut off a rumble in my chest and step into her path.

"Do those guys give you trouble a lot?" The question comes out gruff. Something about catching her surrounded by Mike and his friends rankles me fiercely. "Tell me and I'll put an end to it."

Her shoulders tense, a flush creeping up her neck. She purses her lips and shakes her head. "It doesn't matter."

It doesn't—? My hands flex.

Working my jaw, my gaze sweeps over her while she toys with the cuffs of the sweater she's swimming in. She's on the taller side with long legs, coming up to my chin, though she tends to bundle herself in these big sweaters. She's the perfect height for me to dip my head and kiss the top of her head. That's not something I've done before, yet I picture doing it to her.

Admittedly, I didn't notice her much since I first met Theo. She keeps to herself. My head's always been full of hockey and not much else.

But I noticed her today when she needed someone. I'm seeing her now, worrying her heart-shaped lips with her teeth. I wrap a hand around the strap of my gear bag to keep a tight leash on the urge to stop her and swipe my thumb over her lip to soothe it.

Now that I'm aware of her, I can't make myself walk away. Not without knowing she's got someone watching out for her.

Despite my life revolving around hockey and every one of my goals focused on making it to the NHL, some part of me won't be satisfied unless it's me protecting her.

"Yes it does." At my insistent tone, she peers up at me with big brown eyes. "Tell me if they're bothering you. If anyone does. Okay?"

She blinks in disbelief, blurting out a rushed answer when I step into her, ready to press until she agrees. "Um, yeah. Okay."

I exhale with a nod. "Good."

Studying me as if I'm some wild beast that could

turn on her at any moment, she edges back slowly. "I'm just gonna go now." I follow her again. After a moment, she gives me a wary sidelong glance. "Don't you have practice? You'll be late."

"Yeah. I'll get there after I walk you where you're going."

"Your coaches won't like that." She lowers her voice to impersonate someone that sounds suspiciously like her brother. "Hockey is about attitude. A team works when everyone shows up and respects the game."

A chuckle slips out of me, fogging the air in front of me with my breath. "Is that supposed to be Theo? That was good."

"The game doesn't have emotions, so I think it's pointless to respect it," she says frostily. "It's ridiculous. There are far more worthwhile, *respectable* endeavors in life than speeding around ice with knife boots, chasing around a hunk of rubber, slamming into people, and going insane when the rubber makes it in the net as if it's the greatest achievement ever."

"Not a fan of hockey?" At her dour glance, I find the corners of my mouth curling up. She's cute when she's not hiding herself, even as she hates on the game I've loved since I was a kid, the one I want to make my professional career. "Noted."

Despite being friends with her brother, I don't know her well. She's intriguing.

Quiet falls between us as we walk around campus. Several people wave when they spot me and I shoot them easy smiles. The more people that notice us, the more she ducks her head over the stack of books and flyers in her arms.

"You don't have to walk with me," she says.

"Here." I stop her by a bulletin board and tear down some of the colorful print outs with expired dates from before winter break. "You need to put those up, right? This is a good spot."

Lainey's eyes bounce between her flyers and the space I made for her advertisement. She seems to psych herself up, scanning the area and scrutinizing the flyer before inching toward the bulletin board. I incline my head in encouragement when she glances over her shoulder and tucks her hair behind her ear.

"It's fine. Everyone puts stuff up here. Job offers. Study groups. Events. Look, a Netflix and chill club is looking for members. Well, I hope it's more about binge watching than *chill*-chilling, right?" I wrinkle my brows in thought, reaching for her books. "Let me hold these for you so you don't have to balance them."

She slides her lips together, then the nervous tension bleeds away, stealing my breath with it when it's replaced by determination. Picking a spot not quite front and center, she freezes.

"I didn't bring anything to hang them with," she admits softly, deflating.

I don't like the way it kills off the steady build of conviction. Snagging one of the abandoned push pins, I offer it to her.

"Use this."

She stares at it for a beat before carefully taking it. Her fingers are colder than mine. The quick brush stirs warmth in my chest as I watch her light up with her returning determination. She holds her flyer in place on the board and I skim what it says.

"What's this dance for?"

"Charity. All the proceeds from ticket sales will go to the Derby Bookshop." A sigh leaves her. "I have a lot to do. It was all my idea to organize this. I don't want to see it close its doors in favor of a chain store. I thought the students could help give back to the local community. It's a store that's been there forever."

Stepping back, she admires the flyer, lit up over completing a task so simple that I wouldn't have thought twice about doing. That weird thought about kissing the top of her head is back.

"That's cool. I can take some of those with me to

hang up, if you want. We can cover more ground between the two of us."

"Thank you. For your help, er—" She squints at me, visibly stumped. "You're nice, I suppose."

"You suppose," I echo with a smirk. "I'll be your flyer hanging wingman anytime you need me, sweetheart."

It rolls off my tongue easily.

One thing that gives me an edge when I'm on the ice is my tenacity. Once I put my mind to something, I'm all in.

The instinct to act as her stand-in boyfriend to get those guys to leave her alone rises once more, a plan forming in my head as quickly as I select play strategies to dominate with my team for the W.

I will protect Lainey Boucher from creeps and anyone else who dares to try anything with her by posing as her boyfriend. No one will go after her if they believe she's dating me.

"The team's parties usually start around nine after the game," I say. "I'll get your ticket for you after practice so you can come to watch it, then I'll give you a ride from the arena after I'm done in the locker room. It'll help our cover story if we show up together."

"What?" She whirls on me, the flare of confidence

fading again. "What are you talking about? Why would I do that? I don't go to hockey games."

"Not even to support Theo?" I lift a brow. "He's your brother."

"And? My Dad supports him plenty. He goes to his games." Her jaw works. "And my mom."

She hugs her stuff to her chest and I fight back the offer to carry the books for her the rest of the way, which is odd since I've never done that for any girl I've been with. I don't really have time for girlfriends thanks to the rigorous schedule that comes with being a hockey player. If I'm with a girl, it's not serious. A hookup, maybe two, then I move on. My focus is on making it to the NHL.

I've never allowed anything to distract me from that.

This feels different, though. It's not like we need to devote time to a relationship, which is why girlfriends haven't worked out for me. This would just be an act to help her out.

Lainey sighs. "I don't see why I should go to the game, and I don't plan to be at your party."

"You'd make your boyfriend fly solo after a win?" The corner of my mouth tugs up. "That's cold, babe."

"You're not my—no one will buy that."

She's pretty when she's flustered. Her cheeks turn

pink as she tries to speak all her thoughts at once. I find myself smiling again, a chuckle huffing out of me.

"Why wouldn't they?" I counter.

"They just wouldn't. They'll see through it in an instant. We're too different. You're—*you*," she insists, licking her lips as her gaze lingers on my mouth, dipping down my jaw to my shoulders, landing on my hands rubbing together to keep them warm. She trails off for a moment, watching the prominent veins on the back of them. "And I'm... Well, we're just not compatible. Hello, the age old jock and nerd divide."

"Divide?" I swipe a hand over my mouth to hide my amusement. "Sounds serious."

"Exactly. I'm glad you understand. Thanks again for your help." With a decisive nod, she spins on her heel and continues down the sidewalk. Grudgingly, she adds, "See you around."

I catch up before she gets far and fall into step with her effortlessly. "So, I'll text you a ticket if that works for you."

She jolts. "Have you taken too many pucks to the head? Falls on the ice? Maybe you've had your face smashed into those big windows that keep you separate from the audience and are suffering long-term concussive effects."

"The glass and the boards," I supply. "Do you want

an extra ticket so you can bring a friend? Just not a guy. I get jealous easily. The boards wouldn't stop me if my girlfriend showed up with someone else."

She gapes at me, failing to suppress a shiver at the gravelly edge I let creep into my playful warning. "Why? I don't even know you."

Part of me is wondering the same thing. Yet the protectiveness I felt is undeniable. My gut tells me this is the right call to make.

I lay a hand over my chest. "Don't be like that. I've been your brother's best friend for the last five years. I've been to your house. Heard you baby talk to your dog."

Her eyes go round and her mouth pops open. "This is insane, though." She drops her voice to a whisper. "Who pretends to date? Outside of books where this would make sense, this will go all wrong. A nerd and a hockey player? It's a disaster waiting to happen."

"Your dance is in two weeks, right? We'll keep this easy and fake it until then." I lift my brows. "I want to do this for you. If word gets around on campus that you're dating me, people will back off. Win-win. You get to plan your fancy dance in peace."

Lainey stares at me with wide brown eyes. "You really have taken too many hits to the head."

I laugh at her hushed words. "I'm a man who goes after what he wants, that's all. Are we doing this?"

Lainey throws her hands up. "You know what? Fine. I have too much to do to stand here arguing with you about this all day." She closes the small distance between us and prods at my chest with a finger. "The only way I'm agreeing to this crazy plan is if you'll stay out of my way. *And* you have to break the news to my brother if you're insisting I go to that party. If I do it, he'll know we're lying to everyone."

I grin in triumph. "Deal. One more thing."

"What else could there be?" A worried look crosses her face like she's in the deep end before we've started this.

Smirking, I pass a sweeping glance over her head. A few more people have spotted me. It's the perfect opportunity to get things going. Rubbing the thick sleeves of her knit sweater, I capture her gaze, feeling out how far she's comfortable to take this. When I slip an arm around her waist, she stiffens awkwardly, but allows it. With the same careful slowness and gentleness, I trace the soft curve of her face.

I tilt her chin up, enjoying the way her beautiful heart-shaped lips part. "Can I kiss you?"

"You—what?" she breathes, remaining frozen. "Now? Why?"

Because for some reason, I want to.

"Couples kiss. It'll make it easier to sell this if we go all in with it," I explain. "I don't do shit by halves."

Four years ago, I stayed with the Bouchers in the summer before Theo and I were due at the hockey camp I met him at. I ran into her in the middle of the night when I got up for a drink. She was wide awake, a book tucked under her arm with her place held by a second book sandwiched between the pages, the bottom of an old oversized Flyers hoodie skimming her long bare legs. She was completely lost in her own world and I stood there watching until she left, not once aware of me hovering in the shadows at the edge of the kitchen.

The memory strikes me as I stare at her. I thought about what it would be like to kiss her then, even though her brother would lose it if I tried anything.

I forgot about the fleeting encounter until now. It was the only time I was really conscious of her in the time I've been friends with Theo.

But I think that would put her defenses up if I was honest. She's got a whole thing about how she sees herself in another world than me.

Dipping my head, I ghost a question over her lips. "You want two weeks of peace, don't you? Let me help. It's just a kiss."

Her eyes flicker. "Can I ask you something first?"

"Yeah."

"Do you think people will want to go to my bene-fit?" Her voice carries a hint of self-consciousness, fragile like a thin layer of ice. "I keep having this thought that everyone will think it's silly and no one will show up."

My heart clenches. The fierce burning sensation from earlier returns with a vengeance, tearing through my chest. I want to take her doubt away. I rub my thumb back and forth across her chin.

"Yeah. It sounds fun. I bet you'll sell a lot of tickets." I swipe the tip of my tongue along my lip, guiding her closer until there's no space left, her books trapped between us. "I'll help you."

Relief softens her features, her lashes fluttering. "Okay, fine. You can kiss me. Make it quick."

The corner of my eyes crinkle and I duck down, pressing my lips to her cheek, barely grazing the corner of her mouth. She makes a tiny noise of surprise. It would take no effort to turn my head and claim her lips.

Heat flares low in my gut as soon as the thought enters my mind, driving me to kiss her like I wanted to four years ago. I linger to enjoy the feel of her soft skin on mine, then pull back.

To anyone watching it could've easily been mistaken for a real kiss.

She touches her lips, gaze cutting to the side. "I

wouldn't categorize that a kiss."

"They don't know that." I tip my head, indicating the furtive looks of the other students paying attention.

She narrows her eyes and slips from my grasp, moving down the path again with a parting scoff. I send a grin to the sky before catching up with a few long strides.

"Wait. That wasn't the thing I was going to tell you."

"Then why did you kiss me?" she mutters.

The corners of my mouth curl. Now it's a kiss? "Because you're my girlfriend."

"I'm n—"

"For the next two weeks, you are. We kissed to seal the deal, so this is happening. I'll have one of our rookies meet up with you after practice. You'll be at Derby Bookshop?" At her bewildered nod, I pull out my phone and shoot a text to Reeves with directions. He's the most reliable out of the new rookies. "He'll bring you my jersey."

She watches me suspiciously. "Why would I need your jersey? Don't you need it for the game?"

"I'm giving you my alternate. Girlfriends wear their man's number." I wink. Lainey is speechless. "I can't wait to see you screaming for me, baby. I'll score a goal just for you if you do."

The harassed expression she gives me is priceless.

THREE
ALEX

Water droplets fly from my freshly showered hair as I scrub it with a towel and amble through the locker room to my cubby after practice. Once I tug on a pair of boxers, I get my phone from my duffel bag.

Scrolling through my contacts, I find her number still saved.

> **Alex**
> Hey, practice just ended. Keep an eye out for Reeves. Look for the backwards hat.

"We're out," Easton announces.

The talented rookie slings an arm across Cameron's shoulder and messes with his backwards hat. The two of them wrestle good-naturedly.

"Reeves, hold up."

Cameron turns back at my call. I ball up my white and blue alternate colors, then toss it. He catches the jersey against his chest.

"Got it," he says.

"Got what?" Easton glances between us. "Do we need our alternates? I thought Coach Kincaid said regulars."

"Don't worry about it," I say.

Cameron fixes his hat and leaves. Easton follows him out.

Theo emerges from the showers with a towel slung around his waist and sprawls on the bench next to my locker. "I'm starving. Feel like going to my dad's tonight for wings?"

I stare at him like he's crazy. "Before game night? Nah, man."

He frowns. "I don't feel like cooking. I'm fucking beat after Coach Kincaid's new drill sequences."

Our back up goalie leans around me from my other side. "It's your night."

"Don't worry about it, Holland. I'll take his night and cook."

We finish getting dressed and leave the locker room together. I check my phone, but there's no response from Lainey.

On our way back to the house, I unlock it to read a new notification, but it's not from her either. Just some sorority girls tagging me on social media. I type out another text in case she missed my first message.

> **Alex**
> Did the rookie find you? Feel free to practice your cheering for tomorrow night by trying it on 😏

Throughout prepping and cooking enough pasta to feed a house full of hungry hockey players, I leave my phone handy on the island, continuing to tap the screen to see if she answered.

Normally I'm not so hung up on the chase, yet an unfamiliar anticipation keeps tugging at me. Even during practice, when I'm always in the zone on the ice, I couldn't stop thinking about the look on her face when she gained enough confidence to hang her flyers or how her lashes fluttered when she gave me permission to kiss her.

"You waiting for a booty call, Keller?" Jake Brody, one of our d-men, elbows me with a grin. "Got any hot pics of her to share with the class?"

"Shut up, man." I brandish the wooden spoon at him until he backs away. "Why the hell would I do that?"

Theo catches Brody's shoulders on his way into the

kitchen and snorts, taking a seat at the island. "Don't mess with the man making dinner, Brody."

He grunts in response and retreats from the kitchen. I shake my head, willing my heart to stop drumming so hard. Brody's guess made me picture Lainey and I felt the same fierce protectiveness that overtook me earlier rear back to life. I'd never let anyone see photos of her she entrusted me with.

Not that I'm imagining my best friend's sister sending me any kind of sexy photo.

My gaze guts to Theo and I clear my throat.

Except, fuck, I absolutely am. Once the idea is there, I can't stop it. Images flit through my head of how she might look engulfed in my jersey instead of the oversized sweaters she wraps herself in.

I'm supposed to be the one to tell Theo I'm with Lainey now, not fantasizing about her in front of him. I promised her as part of our agreement. Thankfully he's absorbed in the garlic bread I set on the island to cool, unaware of my crisis.

"Dinner's ready," I force out in a rush, grabbing my phone.

"Aren't you going to eat?" Theo calls after me as I make a hasty exit from the room.

"Later," I toss over my shoulder on my way up the stairs.

I don't stop until I'm in my room, leaning against the closed door. Did I just run away? Yep. Am I proud of myself for it? Nope, but my dick is hard from the brief thought of Lainey in my jersey. The irresistible fantasy toys with my imagination, so no fucking way am I going back downstairs to face her brother until I get myself under control.

Closing my eyes, I blow out a husky laugh.

I might not have noticed Lainey Boucher much before, but now that I have there's no going back to being unaware of her.

My phone alerts with a new notification.

Warmth fills me when I see the screen. She finally responded.

> **Alex**
> She lives. Thanks for the proof of life. I was starting to worry something was wrong.

> **Lainey**
> Could've been that you didn't have my number saved right. Maybe you were texting someone else this whole time who was wondering who you were and how you got their number.

I crack a smile, picturing her leveling me with a matter of fact expression to go with her response.

Alex
Good thing I watched you program your number yourself when your dad wanted us all exchanging numbers in case of emergency on move-in day last year. I always wonder what their life is like when I get a text from a rando. Do you?

Lainey
Yes.

Alex
So you got the jersey?

Lainey
Yes.

Alex
Did you try it on?

Lainey
No.

Alex
What are you doing?

Lainey
Reading.

Alex
What are you reading? Is it for class or for fun?

It takes her a while to respond again. She begins to

type, then the bubble disappears. It happens twice more until she answers.

> **Lainey**
> For fun.

> **Alex**
> Yeah? Is it a good read? Should I pick it up?

> **Lainey**
> I don't think it's your vibe.

> **Alex**
> I mean, I don't read a lot, but if you like it I want to try it.

Again, the typing bubble appears and disappears several times. I don't know what's spurring me on to find out about the book she's reading other than the insistent spark of curiosity. One I've never really had when it comes to the girls I hook up with.

Talking to her isn't about getting into her pants. In every one of the few memories I have of her in my head, I've never seen without a book. The only thing I have in my life that relates to that level of interest is hockey, so I want to know what it's like for her to love something as much as I love my sport.

I push away from the door and collapse into a sprawl across my bed, eyes glued to the phone.

> **Lainey**
> I doubt you would. It's a new romance release I had on preorder. We just got the delivery this afternoon.

> **Alex**
> What's it called? Are there still copies? Put one aside for me, I'll pick it up sometime this weekend.

> **Lainey**
> But it's a romance.

> **Alex**
> I can't read romance? Why not? Is it because I'm a guy?

> **Lainey**
> Um, no that's not what I meant...

> **Alex**
> Then because I play hockey?

> **Lainey**
> I didn't think it would interest you.

> **Alex**
> But you like it.

> **Lainey**
> Of course I like it, it's my favorite genre to read!

This time her response is immediate. I can almost

picture her getting as worked up over this as she did when I asked if I could kiss her on the quad only to brush my lips over the edge of her mouth. I swipe a hand over my jaw, imagining what it would be like to do it for real instead of pretending with her.

Alex
If you love reading romance, I want to give it a try. I want to know about something that's your favorite.

FOUR
LAINEY

Alex
Game day 🏒 Going to wipe the ice
with UConn.

Alex
Just finished an early practice. More
of a strategy lecture from our coach to
get us in the zone to hit the ice
tonight. Are you up yet? Don't you
want to wish your boyfriend good
luck, baby?

Alex
Kidding, you don't have to if you don't
want to. But cheer for me when I
score tonight. And don't be surprised
when I point at you. It means I'm
dedicating the goal to my girl. 😉

THESE CHECK INS have been nonstop since yesterday when Alex decided he would be my fake boyfriend. He went quiet late last night, finally allowing me to enjoy my current read in peace. This morning the texts have started up again. When I got up, I found three new messages waiting for me.

Not long into my first Friday class, I nearly choke on my coffee when he sends a question about the title of my book only to let me know he found it—probably on the display I set up yesterday during my shift—less than five minutes later.

Then there's the text with a photo of his newly purchased romance novel ten minutes after.

Followed by his thoughts on the first chapter being interesting when I'm sitting down in my next class.

Interesting.

What does that mean? Does he think it's weird? Is he still reading?

The thoughts continue to pile on one after the other.

Any chance I have of focusing on the rest of my classes for the day flies out the window because I'm worrying about his opinion of romance books based on trying one. Thankfully it's a contemporary book, because I don't know how the hell I'd handle it if he tried something in the fantasy or monster realm.

On my way into the library to meet up with my

weekly study group early in the afternoon, I finally get an answer to the questions I can't stop thinking about.

> **Alex**
> Didn't mean to keep going, but I couldn't stop reading after I finished the first chapter. I'm up to the part where they're caught in the rain after they went on the trail ride.

Someone almost knocks into me when I stop in my tracks, right in the middle of the aisles between the extra work tables on the second floor. It's less distracting up here than the tables at the center of the atrium on the first floor.

"Watch out," the student mutters, sidestepping to get by.

But I'm not paying attention to anything going on in my surroundings.

I'm so surprised by the unfathomable idea of Alex—hot, popular, athletic, *prime example of ideal masculinity* Alex—not only reading a romance, but enjoying it. So shocked that my brain bypasses my default setting to overthink ten responses as a required step prior to replying.

Before I'm aware of it, I've texted back.

> **Lainey**
> You actually like it?

> **Alex**
> It's not weird if I do, right? It's good.
> I'm man enough to admit it. Some
> parts have me grinning like an idiot.

> **Alex**
> I've never felt my face get so hot
> either. They weren't even doing
> anything sexy. Theo and Brody caught
> me reading a few pages during lunch.
> They asked why I was so red. I didn't
> know how to explain to them that this
> guy swung the girl out of the way of
> the wild horse they're training and had
> her pinned to the wall to shield her
> with his body while they were staring
> at each other.

What is happening? My heart beats faster.

On one hand, I know exactly what scene Alex is talking about. It had me kicking my feet and screaming into a pillow last night when I read it. The long stare built the tension between the couple, then the hero's gaze dropped to the heroine's lips and gave me butterflies.

On the other hand, I can't unload all of my excited fangirling over the moment between the couple. Not to him. It's too much.

I jolt when my phone vibrates again in my hands.

> **Alex**
> Shit, is it actually weird?

Biting my lip, I weave through the tables in a hurry until I reach the one my group prefers for its optimal position three spots away from the big arched windows stretching from the first floor to the third. While I carefully line up my phone, books, and annotation supplies I draft and discard several potential responses.

It is strange. Not because it's romance—the genre is amazing and deserves so much more recognition than it gets. I'm torn by my love of my favorite books and the confusion that I'm talking about them with a hockey player.

> **Lainey**
> No. Romance is for everyone. I was just surprised someone like you would be interested in it.

> **Alex**
> Like me?

> **Lainey**
> You know what I mean.

> **Alex**
> Your boyfriend? 😳

Heat races across my cheeks.

He's not my—

"Hey, you beat me here."

I hide my phone against my chest, emitting an embarrassing shriek. The yell echoes through the quiet library, drawing the eyes of other students here to study.

Caught out, I peek over my shoulder to face Maya Donnelly. She's a freshman I've grown close to since we share an advisor in the psychology department that paired us up.

She huffs out a friendly laugh, joining me at the table. "Whoa, deep breath, girl. I didn't mean to scare you."

"Sorry," I stammer as I cram my phone into my over-stuffed bag. "I was in my own world. I didn't hear you coming up behind me."

"All good." She checks her phone and sets up a focus timer before unpacking her study materials. "Is it just us today?"

The pounding of my heart relaxes.

"I think so. Kelly said she had a meeting with her professor when I saw her before my last class."

She hums, pulling her chestnut brown hair back with a blue flower claw clip. We settle into a comfort-able silence and begin studying. It takes me longer than usual to absorb the key points in my notes, but once I make it through a few pages I manage to lose myself in the methodic drag of my highlighters.

When Maya's phone vibrates, it signals the end of our first twenty minute productivity block. She shoots me a smile and stretches. I set aside the notes I reviewed, then reach for my phone to check the reading assignment for another class. There's a message waiting on the screen.

> **Alex**
> Still there?

How am I supposed to face him tonight? It was crazy enough for anyone to think we're together when he proposed the idea yesterday, when I thought he was just another hockey player. Now he's a hockey player who's buddy reading a cowboy romance with me.

The two Alex Kellers don't fit in my mind. Both are my complete opposite. And fake relationship or not, I definitely don't belong next to him.

> **Lainey**
> I'm studying. My group meets in the library at the end of every week. Actually, I might miss tonight. I should've told you before you bought the tickets for me. We have a lot of work to get through.

> **Alex**
> The game isn't for hours. If you're still working after that long, you'll need a good study break.

No matter what excuse I try to give as a reason I don't really need to go to the game tonight, he isn't giving me an out.

"Ready to go again?" Maya asks.

"Okay. What are you focusing on next?"

She waves a half-filled notebook page. "My summer schedule."

"You're still deciding what to take?"

One of the first things Maya told me when we started getting to know each other was that she wanted to finish her degree in three years. We share that goal. I've been helping her with my tips on managing the heavy course loads.

"Unfortunately." She sighs ruefully. "I've got a summer job lined up to cover my room and board expenses, so I'm trying to plan around that. I can't decide if it's better to front load my prerequisites or go for some of the labs offered for the shorter summer courses."

I hold out a hand. "Let me see."

She passes me her notebook and we scroll through

the available classes for the two summer sessions Heston offers. I tap my pen over one that jumps out at me.

"This one for sure if you plan to take Nelson and Yang's classes your sophomore year."

"Okay, thanks." Maya writes it down, then scans the page. "Then I can do this one on Tuesdays and Thursdays. Perfect."

Her triumphant smile is contagious. We both thrive on these successes in our academic pursuits. It's one of the reasons we get along so well. I might not have many friends at Heston, but having someone like her who I'm comfortable around is enough for me.

"I'm going to submit this to the advisor to check over," she says. "Can you set up the next timer?"

"Sure."

While I'm doing it, the notification bar appears at the top of my phone screen.

> **Alex**
> Don't forget to dress warm for tonight. It gets chilly in the arena. My jersey will be warm but you should wear a hoodie or something underneath.

> **Alex**
> Actually, do you need to borrow one of mine? I can meet up with you.

> **Lainey**
> Thanks, it's okay. I know to dress in
> warm layers.

It's been a long time, but I haven't entirely forgotten what it's like to be at a hockey game when I used to go to see my brother play.

Before I put my phone away, he sends a photo. I roll my lips between my teeth at the hastily drawn red arrows over a screenshot of the Heston University sports arena seating chart. It's surprisingly sweet for a hockey player with a heartbreaker reputation like his.

> **Alex**
> Wasn't sure if you know where you're
> going. I circled your section and row
> where your seat is. I'm heading over
> there now with Theo.

Another photo comes through. My stomach bottoms out, pleasant tingles spreading through my core.

Alex's selfie of him in his pregame suit is—*hot*. So damn hot. How is it possible for him to look even more handsome cleaned up in nice dress clothes?

Every eloquent word I know leaves my head, leaving no thoughts other than admiration for the curve of his smirk.

My fingertips graze the corner of my mouth where

he pretended to kiss me. I can still feel the warmth of his body seeping into mine and the gentle brush of his lips against my skin.

Suppressing a shiver, I smack my phone down on the table and cover it with my notebook so I won't be tempted to look at his photo again. Several people throw pointed glances my way. I forgot where I was for a moment.

I offer an apologetic expression and bury my nose in my nearest book, forcing Alex Keller's perfectly shaped, tempting mouth from my mind.

The rest of my study session with Maya passes uninterrupted.

"I think my brain has officially turned to mush," she says. "I can't take in any more information. Want to call it a day?"

"Already?" I peer out the window at the fading winter sunlight. "I might stay a little longer."

It's easier to stay here in one of my safe spaces than think about what I'm doing tonight. And insanely enough...I think I'm going through with it.

Alex went through the trouble of getting me the tickets and going out of his way to show me where I'd be in the arena so I have a visual. He's putting all this effort in for me when I didn't ask him to.

The least I can do is show up. Even if his plan is

bound to fail. There's no way we're fooling anyone into thinking he sees something in a nerd like me. I swallow the anxiety creeping up my throat.

It's only one night. If I get through it with him, then all I have to focus on is planning my benefit.

So I'll go to the hockey game and wear his number.

"Come on. It's almost time for dinner. You can't stay in the library." Maya starts to pack up her things. "You know what, we should go see a movie."

"Oh," I say haltingly. "Um. I can't, sorry!"

"Oh. No worries." The edge of Maya's mouth lifts in a half smirk. "Got a hot date?"

"No. Well..."

Maybe I should tell her about Alex's plan. My face grows flushed and I fiddle with making the stack of books at my elbow even. Her brows wiggle.

"I'm supposed to go to the hockey game," I admit.

She's surprised. I'm still processing it, too.

"Hockey?" Her voice goes somewhat flat and she busies herself with the last of her notes. "Oh. Have fun."

"I have an extra ticket." I reach for her like a lifeline. "Want to come with me? There's a party after at the hockey house. Please come."

She pats my hand and gives me a soft smile. "I'm sorry. I can't. But you'll have fun! Go cheer for your brother."

And Alex.

"Right." I sigh and gather my things. "See you later."

As if Alex senses I need another check in, my phone lights up with a text from him.

It's another photo. He's in a locker room, dressed in his gear for the game. His smile tugs up the corners of his mouth, forming a dimple in his cheek that my fingers want to trace.

After a moment of hesitation, I reply without analyzing the butterflies in my stomach.

Lainey
See you tonight.

Lainey
Good luck.

FIVE
ALEX

THE SOUND of the arena at game time always injects adrenaline straight into my veins. Tonight's no different. I glide across fresh ice with Theo trailing me for our warm-up. We wave to the people in the crowd shouting our names, though I don't offer more than friendly appreciation for the support to the girls pressing themselves against the glass.

I spot Lainey in the student section near our net. She's the only person in the front row hovering by her seat with an uncertain expression while other students holler enthusiastically as the players run through pre-game drills. She has her arms folded tightly across her chest, though it doesn't do much to hide the fact she's wearing my number.

Damn. An unexpected pulse of heat tugs low in my

gut. It's crazy how good she looks in it. I joked about her wearing it, but I wasn't prepared for how much I'd like seeing her rocking my number, wearing *my* jersey. Reality is better than I imagined last night.

Fake girlfriend or not, when a girl wears a guy's clothes it wakes up a primal side of us that's really fucking into it.

Just like the night I caught her in nothing but an old Flyers hoodie in her kitchen. The memory merges with the fantasy that hit me last night, my mind supplying the idea of her in nothing by my jersey. A low groan leaves me as I refocus my thoughts before my cock hardens at the mental image.

We've been texting since I finished practice yesterday after I instated myself as her fake boyfriend. Or rather, I've been texting her and she's occasionally responded with frazzled answers trying to find any excuse not to come tonight. It's the longest conversation we've ever had. I feel like I know her better than I did yesterday.

I wasn't sure if she'd show up for the game, but she's here.

Her eyes meet mine and my grin widens. She looks away just as quickly. I'm not the only one noticing her. Some nearby fans seated in her row have spotted her in my alternate jersey and have struck up a conversation. I recognize the sorority sisters from the Pi Kappa Alpha parties.

"Give me a pass," I call to Theo when she turns her attention back to me.

We line up for a shoot out drill and he directs the puck to me.

Once it flies into the net, I flash her a grin. My brows lift and I silently ask her *see that, babe? That shot was for you.* Her brows furrow, as if she's saying *big fucking deal.*

I laugh at how unimpressed she is, puckering my lips to blow her a playful kiss. She huffs and waves shyly.

"Who do you keep smiling at like that? You'd better focus on warming up." Ice sprays my feet as Theo skates to a halt abruptly at my side. He stares at his sister in the audience. After a stretch of silence, he mutters, "Damn. Lainey never comes to watch. Hell must be frozen over. She'd better not bring us any bad luck."

There's no one more superstitious than hockey players. Any slight change can be a bad omen or the start of a winning streak. I feel good about her being in the crowd tonight.

"She's here for me," I say at the same time he recognizes that she's wearing my alternate jersey.

My best friend's head whips to me, glaring. "What the fuck is going on?"

Ah, shit. I probably should've thought that one through better. I was too busy getting Lainey to agree to my plan to consider that her terms meant I'd have to lie to Theo and be the guy dating his sister. There wasn't a good time to tell him, but I should've so he didn't find out on the ice minutes before the game.

I hold my gloved hands up in surrender. "I invited her when I ran into her yesterday before practice."

He clenches his jaw and both of us fall into a routine we know well. Pre-game warm-ups have been our own ritual since we started playing together. It's how we find our rhythm to stay in sync as wingers on the first line. He slams his stick down on the ice harder than usual.

I watch him for a moment as he flicks the puck back and forth with quick movements that broadcast his agitation before positioning myself where he sends the pass. *Send* is putting it nicely. He rockets the damn puck at me. If I didn't know him as well as I do after five years of training together, I would've missed it by a mile.

We both watch my slapshot zip into the net. He sends the next three passes even faster. Each time I connect, I grit my teeth. Coach will lose his shit on us if he looks over here. He can smell it a mile away when we're fucking around instead of taking the game seriously. During practice is bad enough, but right before a game starts? Death wish.

"Dude," I bite out after I make the last one, scooping up another puck with the edge of my stick to pass to him. "What the hell?"

Theo narrows his eyes. "You've never hung out with her before. You don't know her. Why are you talking to my sister? Why's she wearing your shit?"

All I picture is her expression as Mike and his dickhead friends closed in on her yesterday. I clench my teeth, my grip choking my stick. "Am I not allowed to talk to my girlfriend?"

Again, I should've thought my answer through before the words flew out of my mouth because my best friend's eyes grow wide, then harden. Maybe Lainey has a point about my cognitive health.

"*Girlfriend?* You? What the fuck do you mean you're dating my sister? She's not some jersey chaser like the girls you normally fu—" Theo cuts off when one of the hotshot rookies skates between us, stealing the puck mid-pass. "Blake!"

Easton flashes him an unapologetic grin after he takes his shot on the net. "Aw, man. Too slow."

It's no secret he's gunning for first line. He's wasting no time, putting in as much work as he can to prove himself not only to Coach Lombard, but to the team that he's got what it takes. As a forward, he's fast as fuck and he's got an edge when it comes to split second decision making. I recognize it because it's similar to my play style. His skating inspires me to make plays that get him the puck to score.

Turning back to Theo, I offer an explanation that will placate him for now. "It's new. Very new. She's different. I'm taking things at her pace and she didn't want to tell you."

He holds his anger, staring me down. "If you fucking hurt her in any way—"

"I wouldn't ever hurt her." The force of my growled response startles both of us. We never fight. I incline my head. "Sorry. I mean it, though."

Theo sighs. "Alright. Whatever."

We finish our drills before it's time for the face-off. Both of us take our positions while our linemate Putnam skates to center ice against UConn.

Once the puck drops, I give myself over to the game. UConn's center wins the face-off. He doesn't make it far into our zone before Theo steals the puck. Our stands erupt in cheers when he pulls off a tight turn and passes to our captain, both of us flanking to support Putnam on either side of the ice.

He catches my eye and signals me. I'm ready for his deke.

Putnam feints a pass to Theo before he dumps the puck into UConn's zone once he crosses the red line. I skate my ass off to chase it down and reach it before their defense reacts. Momentum is on my side and I grin when I pick up the puck first to maintain possession. The d-man closest to me curses, hot on my tail after I skirt around him.

There are two potential paths to a goal right in front of me. Either I take a shot on the goal, or I pass back to Putnam as he pushes into the attack zone.

Before I reach the opening in their defense, UConn's huge defenseman checks me, sending us against the boards.

"Not so fast, you little shit," he barks.

He's a big fucking dude, but I won't let him take the puck. I look for Putnam while faking a struggle to find the weak point in his form. Smirking once I manage to break away from the guy on me, I flick the puck to our center.

Putnam takes the shot and the lamp lights up with the first goal for Heston.

"Yeah!" I shout.

I catch Lainey's eye and her expression knocks into

me harder than UConn's behemoth defense player that tried to keep me pinned against the boards. Her amazement isn't like the blur of faces in the crowd—it's in sharp focus, piercing me. My gaze dips to my number emblazoned across her chest and satisfaction burns through me.

When she recovers with a radiant smile, I'm unprepared. Utterly unequipped for the way my heart squeezes.

A Heston defenseman skates around me to herd me back up the ice, breaking me out of the moment.

Once I have my focus back on the game, something's different. I feel more aware of the players around me, of myself. I'm skating faster, handling the puck, and seeing plays with precise clarity. Maybe I was right about Lainey. She feels like a good luck charm that makes me play better.

By the end of the final period, I've been off and on the ice for two more shifts, switching out with the other lines throughout the game. I've always loved the sound of the stadium filled with the screaming fans and the blades carving up the ice. Yet I'm pumped like never before.

Tonight I'm on fire, and each time I've dominated the ice during my shift, I've felt Lainey's eyes on me. It draws my attention back to her, my heart hammering hard.

When we win thanks to the goal Theo puts up to take our score to 4-1 before the clock runs down, all our guys rush the ice. Blake barrels into my side, Reeves jostling into my other. I bump fists with Theo, his attitude from warm-ups washed away by the win.

Then as I skate around the rink, the cheering of the crowd pales in comparison to the way my chest feels once I lock eyes with Lainey because she's smiling right at me.

SIX
LAINEY

IF I THOUGHT GOING to the hockey game was a feat of madness, walking into the after party to celebrate Heston's win holding Alex's hand is a clear sign I've lost it. The noise is deafening once the people hovering inside the entry hall see us. Alex responds with equal enthusiasm, receiving back slaps and fist bumps. He doesn't let go of my hand, keeping me tucked against his side, providing me with a buffer between me and everyone else.

I search for the girls I met at the game that sat in the same row as me. Even though I was there by myself and not part of their group, they were surprisingly nice. Once they realized I was alone, they included me, celebrating every great play with me like we were friends.

My stomach sinks when I don't see them on our way through the house where most of the team lives.

Maybe they'll come later. I cling to the hope of something familiar to latch on to. It's the only way I'll get through a party with the hockey team.

Alex squeezes my hand and leads me to the kitchen where we congregate around an island. "Want a drink?"

I shake my head. He accepts a bottle of water from the freshman who warmed up with Alex and Theo.

"Thanks, E."

I watch Alex's throat bob as he chugs half of it, transfixed by the corded muscles. "You don't drink?"

He shrugs. "I do. I have to keep a pretty strict diet to stay in peak condition. Coach doesn't let us get too wild. Somehow he always knows."

Easton snorts. "He's psychic. Either that, or he's got the house bugged."

Alex pulls a face. "The shit we get up to here? I hope not."

I swallow, curious if he means how many girls have been in his bed. Then my brain helpfully supplies that my brother lives here, too. I grimace.

Easton covers a laugh with his fist and nods to me in greeting. "Hey, I'm Easton." He offers a lopsided grin. "Number twenty-four."

"Hi." I remain glued to Alex's side.

"This is my girl, E." He drops my hand in favor of sliding his arm around me, his large hand encompassing the dip in my waist. I'm distracted by the way he massages it with a little squeeze before dragging his hand down to rest over my hip. "Lainey, this is one of our rookies."

"You left off very promising." He dodges the empty water bottle Alex chucks at him, ending up circling the island to my side. He tilts his head. "You look sorta familiar."

"Ever heard of twins?" Theo enters the kitchen from behind us and shoots Alex, then me a tense look.

A muscle jumps when he locks his jaw before rummaging in the fridge for a sports drink. Alex's arm tightens around me.

Easton snaps and points between me and my brother. "Oh shit, yeah. That's wicked."

"Is that Keller in the kitchen? Get in here!" someone shouts from the next room.

Alex peers over my head. "Want to come with me, or hang out in here?"

"Go ahead." I accept the water Eason gets out of a cooler for me. "It's less people-y in here. I'm acclimating."

The corner of his mouth kicks up. He spares Theo a glance before leaning in to kiss my cheek. His lips brush the edge of mine, the same as the first time he kissed me. I squash the urge to stiffen—and the temptation to press against him, intoxicated by the heady, masculine scent he surrounds me with.

PDA. Right. That's a thing couples do.

His lips linger longer than a quick peck. He pulls back far enough to meet my gaze.

"I don't want to leave you alone, sweetheart," he murmurs. "I won't be long. If you feel up to it, don't be afraid to find me before I come back for you."

"Okay."

He closes the distance between us once more to kiss my forehead. This kiss only lasts a moment before he leaves. I hear the boom of his voice and his laughter when he enters the next room. Easton follows him, leaving me alone with Theo.

"Why didn't you tell me you were hanging out with Alex?" He stares at me. "You didn't have to go behind my back."

"How am I going behind your back?" I stall, unsure what I should say about the cover story. Screw it. I'll go with what's closest to the truth. "It just happened with Alex. I didn't know I needed to tell you anything about it."

He sighs. "Look, Lainey, he's—"

"Your best friend," I snap.

"Yeah, but that's not what I meant. I just don't want you to get hurt because he sleeps around with a lot of girls."

I narrow my eyes, tearing at the water bottle label. "I'm well aware of his reputation. And his sexual history, since I'm his girlfriend." Only one of those statements is true. I roll with it since it makes my brother's face pale. "It's not really your business, Theo. So back off."

He holds his hands up. "I just want to know why neither of you thought you could say anything to me."

I open my mouth with another fierce retort ready to defend my made up actions with Alex, then close it. "I didn't want to make anything awkward if it didn't last."

Because it won't last. This is only for two weeks until the benefit.

Theo's brow wrinkles, but he seems to accept the answer. Annoyed, I spin on my heel and march into the next room to find Alex. He's leaning over the back of a couch facing a large flatscreen TV, laughing. I stop once it occurs to me I walked willingly into the crowded party.

He spots me and holds out an arm in invitation. Keeping my head down, I put one foot in front of the other until I'm within reach. He guides me to stand in front of him, his chest pressing against my back as he braces his hands on either side of me on the couch.

"Why play virtual hockey? You just played a game," I point out.

He chuckles in my ear. "Love of the game. Losing team has to stay sober and cook breakfast tomorrow."

I feel like the center of attention situated in the middle of the room with only the couch and Alex as my shields, but no one's staring at me like I'm out of place.

This isn't as hard as I pictured, though. All we're doing is standing around while attached at the hip. He hasn't made me sit on his lap or actually kissed me. I can do this whole fake girlfriend thing.

My stomach dips when his arms wrap around me in a hug, his chin resting on my shoulder. He's warm and I'm aware of the hard lines of his body everywhere he touches me. I don't know if he's doing it on purpose, but his hand splays against my torso and caresses me every few minutes. He doesn't move lower or higher, but every brush of his fingertips makes my pulse pound between my thighs.

"Excuse me," I blurt when my entire body tingles with overstimulation. "Bathroom."

Alex holds on for a beat longer before releasing me.

"Upstairs, to the left," Easton says without breaking

eye contact with the screen while he smashes buttons. "Damn you, Reeves. That was a cheap shot."

His teammate chuckles. "It worked, didn't it?"

I slip away and find my way to the front door to catch my breath. Cool air hits me when I step out on the porch and lean against the door. My eyes close and I sigh.

A soft meow sounds at my feet. I peer down to find a cat stretched out in front of a bowl of water. It gets up and twines around my legs with another faint cry.

"Hello."

The cat presses into my ankle, purring louder while it rubs against my calf. It calms the rapid pace of my anxious pulse until I breathe easier. It's chilly out, but I like the stillness of the night air.

"I'd rather be here with you than in there," I murmur to the cat when I take a seat on the porch steps.

It responds with a talkative trill that makes a smile tug at my lips. I'm not seated more than a few seconds before the cat helps itself, climbing on my lap. It bumps its head against my chest to ask for more attention. I oblige, stroking the cat's back.

"Your fur's very soft for a stray."

"It should be. Easton is always out here brushing her."

I jolt at Alex's deep voice behind me. Rather than

drag me back inside to his party, he sits next to me, offering his fingers to the cat, holding still while she sniffs him.

"She keeps coming around because he feeds her," he says. "He's got the rest of us doing it, too. She's basically claimed this place as hers now."

As he explains, he gives the cat plenty of affection. She flops on my lap to show him her belly, purring so loud that I feel the vibrations in my legs.

"I didn't hear you come out," I say.

"Did it get to be too much in there? You can tell me if you need a break." His eyes lift to meet mine.

My stomach dips from his unwavering attention. "I told you I don't go to parties."

"I'm glad you came." He nudges his knee against mine. The warmth cuts through the cold night. "Did you like the game?"

My usual refusal of all things hockey sits on the tip of my tongue. Instead I swallow it back because it's not true. Once upon a time, I didn't mind hockey so much. Until it stole all the good things from my life.

"I had fun. You're really good at it."

He smirks. "I train hard. I love the game. You should come more often."

"Maybe." I'm not ready to cross that bridge.

"Lainey."

I look up and tense at the sight of Mike and his buddies coming up the walkway to the porch. The cat jumps off my lap and bounds to the edge of the porch.

"Mike." Alex's tone is as even and friendly as always, but there's a hint of something harder lurking beneath.

"Good game." His hard gaze slides back to me. "I guess you're celebrating."

"All night long." Alex hooks his arm around me.

I bite my lip at the implication, peeking at him from the corner of my eye. He stares Mike down while kneading my hip and thigh. Some strange, unspoken masculine battle goes on between them.

"You going inside?" he prompts.

When Mike doesn't move, Alex squeezes my hip twice to signal he's about to do something. I'm impressed I don't make a peep when his fingertips graze my chin to guide my face to his. He smiles before ducking down to kiss the corner of my mouth. Unlike before, his lips move to mimic a deeper kiss. I gasp, and I suppose it sells it because Alex cups my face, emitting a low, gravelly sound that pierces into my stomach.

Mike mutters something, stomping up the steps to go into the party. Alex pulls away with a smug expression once they're inside.

"I'd say our trick play is a success," he rasps.

"You keep doing that," I say when my heart rate slows.

"What?"

I point to the corner of my mouth. "Kissing my cheek instead of kissing me for real."

He grins, planting a hand behind me and dipping his head close to mine. His attention flicks down to my mouth. "You want a kiss, baby? All you have to do is ask."

My lips part and my cheeks grow hot. I almost ask, swept up by the sound he made when he was fake-kissing me.

Then he laughs and I want to swallow my tongue.

"Do you want me to take you home?" Alex offers, holding out a hand once he gets up. "Or do you want to go back inside?"

I stare at his palm as I consider what to do. This hasn't been as hard as I thought it would be to pretend with him. Will a little longer hurt me?

I put my hand in his and allow him to help me to my feet. "Let's go back inside."

If I can pretend to be Alex's girlfriend, I can be a girl who belongs in his world for a little longer.

SEVEN
ALEX

DURING MONDAY MORNING'S early practice, I've decided I'm going to find Lainey on campus after we finish our ice time.

I'm here to work, so I should be focused on hockey and hockey only. Except that's not the case.

Instead of envisioning connecting with the puck and putting it in the net, I keep thinking about Lainey instead. Her cute laugh. The way her dark blonde hair frames her face nicely. How she looked in my jersey cheering from the stands.

Rather than looking forward to going out with my boys or scoring the next goal against our opponents, I'm more interested in finishing the book so I can talk to Lainey about it.

Something warm stirs in my chest every time she

opens up about the things she's passionate about, and I want to know that side of her. She's so lively behind the walls she puts up between herself in the world.

When I walked her home after the party Friday night, I got her talking about the dance she's planning to raise funds that will keep Heston Lake's bookstore family-owned. She grew even more animated and came out of her shell. I found myself smiling like an idiot.

Luckily, UConn didn't have it together for our away game against them on Saturday after their loss the night before, because she occupied my mind more than I want to admit. Theo and Easton were the stars of the game, lighting the lamp relentlessly while I skated on autopilot.

Shaking my head to empty it, I peel off from the technical drill we're practicing to get a drink. I need to get my head back in it, or my name won't show up on the prospects list for the draft. I've worked too hard to lose sight of the level I need to be at to make myself an asset NHL teams want on their roster.

"Good hustle, Keller." Our assistant coach, Cole Kincaid, gives me an approving nod when I skate up to the boards where he's watching us practice.

He started as a new coach after our season was already underway. He's known to push us harder in practice than the head coach does, focusing on fine-tuning our skills to create a stronger foundation we can build on. Some of our players have improved a crazy amount since he joined the Heston U coaching staff.

I duck my head, not feeling like I've earned his praise when I've spent the last twenty minutes on the ice with my mind wandering. All the guys are showing up to put their top efforts in and I should be, too. My teammates deserve my best whenever I'm out there.

That's the kind of athlete I've honed myself to be. I shouldn't let anything distract me from that.

Everything else off the ice doesn't matter right now. It can wait.

Bracing my arms on the half wall circling the rink, I give myself a mental pep talk to get back in the zone. A phone rests at my elbow next to the row of water bottles. It pings, drawing my attention.

Coach Kincaid stiffens, snatching it off the boards before I read the lit up screen. He's usually pretty chill. I lift a brow at the shift in his attitude, squirting another burst of Gatorade into my open mouth.

He hunches over his device, smothering a tortured groan. "*Fuck.*"

I clear my throat, edging away on my skates. Kincaid's gaze snaps up to me as if he forgot I was there taking a drink break. He glances around, opens his mouth, closes it, then shoves his phone in the pocket of his zip up jacket.

"Never mind. It doesn't have to do with hockey. Forget you saw this. Keep at it," he directs in a clipped tone. "I'll be right back."

I move away from the boards to take up my position once again, exchanging a look with Theo and some of the others in our drill group.

"What's up with him?" Theo wonders aloud.

I shrug. "Beats me. He got a text and didn't want me to see it."

"Bet it's a booty call," Brody crows, circling behind me with a hard stop that sprays ice.

"Gossip on your own time. Let's get back to practice," I say. "Theo, you're up with Blake."

"Time to dance." Easton flashes us a grin, then takes off.

Theo follows him. "Not so fast, Blake."

Folding my hands over my stick, I lean my chin on them and track their passing drill with a steady gaze, analyzing every move to apply to my own skill set.

A sharp focus is what will lead me to my goals every time.

EIGHT
LAINEY

TEARING my gaze away from Alex's ass while he lowers the heavy boxes he insisted on carrying for me, I tick another item off my to do list in my journal for the benefit. He threw me off by texting to ask where I was, then showing up freshly showered after his morning practice and offering his help. The last hour has been distracting rather than productive because the soap he uses smells incredible, temptingly fresh and minty.

I'm still not sure why he wanted to spend time with me. Surely going to his game and the party were enough for it to get around that we're dating as far as everyone is concerned. Temporarily.

"That the last one?" He brushes his hands off and saunters over.

The veins of his hands stand out, catching my eye

with their tantalizing shape. Images from the romance book I read late last night flit through my head, Alex's large hands taking the hero's place while he wrapped them around the heroine's hips as he thrust—

"See? Wasn't so bad. If you'd let me call the rookies over, it could've been faster. What's next?"

His earnest tone breaks me out of the fantasy. I shouldn't be thinking about him as the star of the spicy scenes in my books.

"I can do the rest myself," I mumble, cheeks flaming.

"Nah." Alex swipes the journal from me and scans it. "I said we're hanging out the whole day and you accepted. This isn't exactly how I'd show off my boyfriend skills, but we'll make it work. I'm helping."

I huff. "Helping me overheat."

"What?" His gaze slides to me.

"Nothing." I pluck my journal from his hands, satisfied when he gives it up without a fight. "We need to let the maintenance guy know we're done dropping off the table linens so he can lock the banquet hall up."

"Got it. I'll be right back." Alex clasps my shoulder and plants a quick kiss on my forehead. "Meet me in the lobby."

My tongue twists itself into a useless mess and I stare at his back. There wasn't anyone around to see, yet he did anyway. He does this stuff so naturally. Kissing my head, holding my hand—for a guy who isn't known for dating, the boyfriend role suits him.

I cross my arms, wondering if my mom's AHL player was like that to woo her away from her marriage and family. Maybe they're all this smooth.

Sighing, I give the ballroom one last check before maintenance locks up. Alex snags my hand on our way out to the parking lot.

He taps the dashboard clock when we climb inside his truck. "Let's do the tickets now. The quad will be busy with people coming and going for lunch."

My lips twitch into a frown. "I was planning to get the supplies for the book arch that people will enter under next. But you're right. If we're going to maximize ticket sales, then now is an optimal time."

Nodding, he rests a hand on my headrest to back out, handling the wheel with the same ease as he handles his hockey stick. For some reason, it leaves me short of breath.

Alex doesn't let me carry the table or the chairs he packed in the back of his truck. I'm ready to fight him over the bi-fold sign, but he lets me carry it by myself. Once we're set up on the quad between the two biggest dorms on campus, I eye the people passing us with trepidation. This is like the flyers all over again. I feel on display.

"Hey guys. What's up?" Alex's smooth voice cuts through the fear creeping up my throat. He rests a comforting hand on my leg and waves a couple over. "Have you seen the flyers for the Ballgowns for Books event? Tickets are on sale now. You get points for a sweet date night and we're supporting a charitable cause to help a local small business."

The girl's eyes sparkle. "I never got to go to my prom. This sounds awesome. I want to do it."

"We'll take two tickets," her boyfriend says.

"Hell yeah. You're going to have a great time." Alex rubs my leg. "How much do they owe for two, baby?"

I gulp, not sure if my stomach is fluttering from nerves or from his touch. "Fifty-five each."

They hand over their money and nod to Alex. "Thanks. Great game last weekend."

Once they leave, a group of girls buy tickets. Then a guy recognizes Alex and ends up picking up a pair for him and his girlfriend. Within twenty minutes, we have a line. Things move so fast with Alex doing the talking and me handling the money box, my self-conscious anxiety fizzles into background noise, overtaken by the task at hand.

"This isn't what I pictured," I say during a lull. "I didn't know how I was going to get people to come to the table other than the sign, or sell enough tickets to make a difference for the bookshop."

I certainly wasn't going to get up and talk to people like Alex has. A band tightens around my chest. If I care so much about this, why is it so hard to do what he does without overthinking it?

He gives me a carefree shrug. "Once they see there's a line, it's easy. Everyone wants in on whatever's going on."

I've always seen Alex as an extension of Theo. A hockey player I thought was full of himself like all the rest. But he's not what I expected. His charisma and crooked smiles aren't only his weapons for flirting. He's not an aggressive caveman like Mike.

This side of him has challenged my view on hockey players.

"Thank you for helping out with this. You didn't have to."

"This is really important to you," he says.

I nod, twining the cuff of my sweater around my fingers. "I want to bring the magic of reading a great story to life. To walk through its pages and experience the world within. I..."

Hesitation clogs my throat. I bite my lip, gathering the courage to open up about something I never talk about.

"I love books. They're my favorite escape. Derby Bookshop means everything to me. Not just because it's where I work." I keep my eyes on my hands. "It's where I found an outlet after my parents divorced because of my mom's affair. Dad and Theo have always had each other and hockey, but I have my books and a safe place to work hard on my studies."

Silence stretches after I finish speaking. I lift my head and choke back a gasp at the way his green eyes pin me in place beneath their intensity.

"Lainey—"

"Alex? Oh my god, yes!"

We both look up as a trio of friends approach. It's the girls who sat next to me at the game. They wave to him, then light up once they recognize me.

"Ahhh!" The first one who spoke to me when she saw me wearing Alex's number jumps up and down. "Hi! You look so cute. What's this for?"

"The Ballgowns for Books benefit." I'm proud of myself for answering without mumbling. I even made eye contact. "It's a winter formal to support the bookstore next to the coffee shop. The theme is walking through your favorite fairy tales."

"Stop it, that's so cute," her friend gushes. "I'm going to have a Belle moment? Sign me up."

"I'm texting our sorority sisters, they'll definitely

want to hear about it," the third girl says. "We'll grab three tickets, please."

"Thank you," I manage.

"Give us your number, too. Want to get ready with us?"

"Oh, uh. Maybe?" I nudge my phone across the table. "I have to be there early."

"We'll figure it out. Text you later!"

I blink. Did I make friends and not realize?

"Doesn't look like there are that many left. I think we can move those for sure," Alex says once the girls leave.

"What? No way."

Sure enough, when I count what I have left in the envelope, there are less than twenty. Amazed, I count the remaining tickets again. It takes a moment to sink in how successful we've been today.

"We're almost sold out. I doubt I would've sold this many tickets without your help," I admit. "People tend to ignore me. Most days, I like that arrangement just fine. But I was worried when it came to this benefit that no one would care."

"I didn't do anything, sweetheart." He rests an arm across the back of my chair, absently rubbing my shoulder to keep me warm. "This is all you. Hockey isn't the only thing people can get hyped over at this school."

I scoff. "Please. Hockey is *all* people obsess over here." I poke him in the chest. "It makes sense, I suppose. You're all attractive and display nimble skills when you hit the puck around the ice."

"There's way more to it than that." He smirks. "Should I strip off my jacket and shirt? Watch, those last tickets will fly."

I roll my eyes, pressing my palm against his hard body. The shove I give him has little fire in it. His deep, warm chuckle vibrates against my hand and wraps around me. I bite my lip as a rush of heat coils in my stomach, squeezing my thighs together at the decadent sound.

His laughter tapers off and his gaze rakes over me. "Has anyone asked you yet?"

I give him a questioning look. "Asked me what?"

He studies my face for a moment with an expression I don't understand. "Are you going alone?" When I shrug, he hums, nodding slowly. He captures my hand before I pull it away, running his thumb over my knuckles. "I'd like to buy two tickets."

"Oh." Heat floods my cheeks.

Alex, to my surprise, is a good guy. Maybe the only exception to my hockey players suck rule. I don't think I can deny I was wrong about him anymore. He's great... just not *mine*. I forgot.

"Right. Of course." I pull from his grasp and fumble for the money box. "I, um. Appreciate you supporting a good cause. I didn't think you'd be interested in going, let alone bringing someone."

But of course he'd have a date in mind. There's always a swarm of girls around him. Pretty girls that laugh and know all the right things to say to guys like him. That don't get uncomfortable in a crowd and enjoy going to parties to be social.

I swallow thickly and hand over his tickets. He tucks his money in with the other proceeds we've earned.

Another smirk tilts his mouth. It causes a dull ache in my chest.

"Lainey, can I take you to the dance?" Alex murmurs.

My world comes to a stop. It happens slowly as his question registers, then all at once, the universe snapping to a halt.

I take my glasses off and clean them on my sleeve as if the change in perspective will help me process the moment better. When I pop them back on my face, the smudge-free view doesn't change. Alex still has a soft, handsome smile, waiting patiently for an answer.

"What?" The word trips off my tongue. "Why would you do that?"

"Why not?"

Glancing around, I lean close and lower my voice. "I thought we only agreed to fake it until the dance?"

"Right." He takes my hand again.

My brows pinch and I try to ignore how nice it feels. He's acting like my fake boyfriend. He wouldn't hold my hand otherwise.

"So...? That's more than two weeks. And besides, being in your world of jocks and partying is one thing, but pretending in mine is—"

"Don't talk to me about your divide theory again." He dips his head, lifting his brows.

It makes his chiseled jaw look more defined and my insides tangle into a hot, pleasant knot. I can't help but like it when he goes from charming to commanding.

"There's no divide. Have people been assholes today?" He sweeps an arm out. "At the party?"

He has a point. The girls seated next to me at the hockey game included me in their excitement without a second thought and absorbed me into their group as if I always belonged. Then at the party, his teammates weren't all that bad. Other than my brother getting in my face, I didn't feel entirely out of place. Only overwhelmed because of my own anxious hangups.

No one singled me out for being a nerd.

Licking my lips, I shake my head. "I don't..."

He smiles again and caresses my hand. "You're

going to your own party, aren't you? You're working hard all on your own to put it together. You're the one who should enjoy it the most."

"I mean, I have to be there to make sure it runs smoothly. I—I have a dress, but—"

He leans in, eyes bouncing between mine. "Go with me. I want to take you."

Eyes wide, I stammer, "O-okay."

"Good."

My heart does a dizzying twirl in my chest at his devastating grin. He lifts my hand and kisses it with a gentle brush of his lips.

When I agreed to his crazy plan to pretend we're together, I mostly wanted him to leave me alone so I could plan my benefit in peace. I didn't think I'd get to know him, that he could make my stomach fill with butterflies and my heart race.

I never expected to feel comfortable around a hockey player as popular as Alex Keller.

Yet here I am, falling into the same trap as every other girl on campus over my brother's best friend. I need to be careful, or I'll end up hurt by this precarious game we're playing.

NINE
LAINEY

With only a short amount of time left to prep before the Ballgowns for Books benefit next weekend, it's crunch time. I'm getting excited to see all of my planning come together, but also nervous that there's only a little over a week left to get it done.

Before I was worried no one would come, but after tickets sold out two days ago with Alex's help, now I face the pressure of making an incredible night to remember.

I have my notes for the dance open on my stock cart while I add more books to the display for the new romance release.

The one Alex has been buddy reading with me. My face flushes.

Technically I've already finished. I stayed up through the night when I first got it and read it cover to cover. I've read two more books since then. He insists that he'll be done by this weekend even though I told him he didn't have to.

I still can't believe he's reading it. The thought of his reactions to the spicy parts keep me up at night, leaving me hot and bothered when I think—*fantasize*—of him doing any of the sexy things the hero in the book does.

No one has to know that I've imagined his thumb tracing my lips before swooping down for a knee-weakening kiss, or his big hands dipping beneath my skirt to explore my body, or whispering praise in my ear that would leave me swooning.

Or hoisting me into his arms, pinning my back to the wall, and encouraging me to wrap my legs around his waist while he—

"Lainey."

I almost jump out of my skin. Whipping around to face Mr. Derby, I adjust my glasses self-consciously.

"Yes?" I squeak.

Hopefully he can't tell I'm blushing. Or what I was thinking about. That would be so weird.

The fondness in his weathered expression reminds me of my dad. "Once you're done with that restock, you can take your break."

I wipe away invisible dust from my maxi skirt and tug the sleeves of my thick sweater over my hands just for something to do with them. Even though I've grown used to working here, the habitual urge to do something with my hands is difficult to break.

"Okay. Thanks. Oh!" He turns back before leaving. "I was wondering if you have any old photos of the store."

"Sure. What for?"

"I had an idea to do a display about the history of the store in Heston Lake for the benefit. I thought it might help garner more interest in preserving it by encouraging people to support a family-owned business."

Mr. Derby gives me a wobbly smile. "Thank you, Lainey. For your hard work and for believing in this place."

I return his smile with a bright one of my own. "Of course. This is my happy place."

"I'll go see about those photos."

"That's one more thing to check off," I murmur to myself in satisfaction.

Leaning over my cart, I tick the box on my list for the photos. I wheel it out of the way as a customer strolls in and pauses by the display. In the back, I tuck my notebook into my bag, then grab my phone and wallet.

There are several texts waiting for me. One's from Maya a few minutes ago asking if I'm taking a break soon because she's on her way to get coffee next door.

The rest are all from Alex. I flatten a hand over my stomach as butterflies rush through it.

> **Alex**
> I was just thinking of you. Have a good day at work.

> **Alex**
> My morning class was hell to sit through. The lecture was legit about to put me to sleep. I stayed up too late reading. No regrets 🤪😂

> **Alex**
> I'm on my way to the gym for a workout with Theo.

Biting my lip, I reply to Maya and hurry out of the bookstore before I read too much into his texts. He's being friendly. That's all.

Maya already has a drink waiting for me when I get to Clocktower Brew House. She waves from the mismatched armchairs by the window where we like to people watch. I weave through the busy coffee shop to join her.

"Hey," she greets over the rim of her latte.

"Thanks for the coffee." I sink into the cushy chair.

She uses a peppermint stick to stir her drink. "No problem. Oh, I heard back from Justine with approval for the classes we picked for my summer semester. She agreed with you that it was a good call."

"That's great. It's such a relief to know your schedule is all sorted, right?"

"Totally. With your help roadmapping it, I feel way better about tackling my credits in three years."

"You've got this." We share a smile. "I wish planning this benefit was as easy as it is to create the perfect class schedule."

"You've done a great job. I seriously wish I could be there to see it all finished. You'd better send me pictures."

My shoulders slump. "I will. It won't be the same without you there."

She was the first person I worked up the courage to invite, but she has plans to visit home for the weekend to see her family. Since I've known her, I've rarely seen her go home and I know it's important to her to visit her grandfather.

"It's going to be amazing. You're going to have such a good night."

I shift my gaze to the window, murmuring, "I hope so."

Maya waves to someone she knows as I finish off my coffee. I check the time on my phone to make sure I'm not taking too long of a break.

Just as the screen lights up, I get a text from Alex. It's a post-gym selfie that leaves me breathless when I open it. He's shirtless, flexing his bicep. His muscles are glistening and he's giving the camera a brazen grin that ignites heat in my core.

> **Alex**
> What do you think? Did I train hard enough? 😅

> **Alex**
> I've got to up my game if the guys in books are all like this Wyatt dude. Don't worry, I'm confident if you're ever stuck in a burning barn I'm strong enough to carry you. Easy.

A flush spreads over my cheeks.

"What's got you smiling like that?" Maya asks.

"Wh—no one," I blurt.

Her eyes widen. Crap.

"*Nothing*," I correct.

"So it's a someone?" The corners of her eyes crinkle. "Do I know them? If not, I totally want to meet them. We should all hang out for coffee."

What I would give to have confidence like hers. She enjoys meeting new people, and she's great at talking to them. I watch her make new friends regularly.

If I was more like her instead of shy and anxious, maybe Alex might actually like a nerd like me.

But we're only pretending.

Before Maya can ask anything else, someone claps their hands down on my shoulder and leans around me.

"I thought that was you. Hey girl!" Candace beams, giving me a little shake.

"Hi," I manage.

"It's so great to run into you. Hi," she says to Maya. "I'm Candace."

"Maya. Nice to meet you."

Candace perches on the arm of my seat, balancing her to-go cup and a croissant while she searches through her purse for her phone. "Oh my god, I have to show you the dress I found for next weekend. My sorority sisters are in love with it. It's so perfect!"

"I can't stay. I'm on my break, but I should probably get back to the bookstore," I admit apologetically. "It's just me and Mr. Derby in today, so I don't want to leave him by himself for too long."

She waves me off. "Oh, no worries at all. I'll text it to you instead."

Since giving her my number, she's invited me on coffee runs with her and she asked for some recommendations to get started reading romance.

"Um. If you're not busy, you could come with me. If

you want." I rise to my feet, twisting the cuffs of my sweater between my fingers. "I've got a list of books for you."

She lights up. "The romance recs? Yes! That's perfect."

"I mean, you don't have to read the whole list. It's pretty ambitious. But you asked for where to start reading, and I got kinda carried away."

"I'll walk back with you, too," Maya says. "Reagan sent me on a mission to get that new cowboy release."

The three of us make our way through the coffee shop.

On our way out, Candace giggles. "You know, I think this is the most you've said to me so far. So the way to your heart is books, got it."

I think this means we're friends. I never would've expected this when we first met at the hockey game. I glance between her and Maya. The corners of Maya's eyes crinkle with her smile. She gives me a thumbs up.

A spark of happiness expands my chest. I tell Candace about the books I included on the list on the short walk to the shop, adding more options off the top of my head when she responds with her own bubbly enthusiasm.

For once it feels easy to connect with someone unexpected.

TEN
ALEX

It strikes me that I'm becoming obsessed when I'm standing on the quad waiting for the three dots floating in my text thread with Lainey to turn into words. In fact, I'm not *becoming* obsessed, I'm already there.

It's time I admit to myself how much I look forward to texting her, thinking about the next time I'll see her, even reading books she likes just so I have more reasons to talk to her.

Hockey has been the only thing to dominate my attention since the first time I held a stick in my hands.

A girl has never come close to competing with my focus on hockey, let alone surpass it.

Yet Lainey occupies all my thoughts after a week and a half. When I'm at practice, weight training, on the team bus for an away game, kicking the rookies' asses on

Playstation, during classes, between classes, eating, *sleeping*—all the fucking time.

I've always kept girls at arm's length, believing they'd be a distraction I couldn't afford. It helped weed out anyone who thought I could give them more than something physical. Sex is an outlet for me. It's fun. Blows off steam. I didn't think I'd care about the other things that make a relationship work—the feelings, thinking about another person all the time, considering their needs before mine.

I never knew it could be like this. Not even when I suggested this fake dating cover as an impulsive excuse to be around her.

Is it weird to go from someone who is strictly hookups only to wanting to spend all my free time with the girl I'm supposed to be pretending to date in such a short time?

Maybe.

Do I care?

Not one goddamn bit.

My boys can bust my balls for it all they want. I'm owning my shit: I'm obsessed with my teammate's sister.

I want to laugh at myself because my heart does an odd squeeze in my chest when she responds.

> **Lainey**
> In the library. I came to study and start my next paper, but I finished that.
> Now I'm working on final BFB prep.

It's only been a handful of days since I last saw her, yet I'm pushing my legs to move faster.

The dopey ass smile on my face is out of my control. Theo would give me so much shit for acting like this if he saw me.

> **Alex**
> Don't go anywhere. My class ended early. I'm heading your way.

> **Lainey**
> Do you need to talk to me about something? You don't have to come to the library. I'll be finished in a little bit.

> **Alex**
> Nah, I just thought I'd come hang out. Spend time with my girl since I didn't get to see you over the weekend 😊
> See you soon.

Our game schedule took us to Minnesota State for a non-conference roadie that we didn't get back from until late Sunday night. The coaches have been working us extra hard in practice since we have a

Thursday home game against Northeastern followed by a rare weekend off coming up at the end of this week.

Tucking my phone away, I hustle to the library. I've never been here.

My major is in communications—something I picked because it's easy to manage since I'm only here as a stepping stone to the NHL. I do the bare minimum required to maintain my eligibility to play. The ice is where my real job happens.

I manage to navigate the main lobby once I swipe my student card to get in. My brows lift at the glass dome over the atrium with four mezzanine floors of bookshelves. In the center of the room, there are tables with students busy at work on their assignments.

Sometimes I forget this is the point of college for most people who aren't here on the athlete track.

It doesn't take long to find Lainey. I hang back for a minute to watch her. Warmth spreads through my chest. I rub at the phantom sensation, stomach tightening.

Lainey is cute. She twirls strands of dark blonde hair around a finger while making notes in her journal. Her glasses sit low on her nose. I'm distracted by the way she sucks her bottom lip into her mouth as she reads.

Rubbing my hands together, I approach her from behind. Powerless to stop myself from indulging in what

I want, I gather her hair to the side and bend to kiss the junction of exposed skin at her shoulder and neck.

She startles with a strangled cry, clapping a hand over her mouth. Wide-eyed, she peers around at the people staring at us from the other tables.

"Sorry," she murmurs.

A chuckle slips out of me as I take a seat beside her. "I didn't mean to give you a jump scare."

She levels me with a sardonic look as she regains her composure, propping her chin on her hand. "And I didn't think any hockey players knew how to find the library."

The corner of my mouth kicks up. Draping an arm across the back of her chair, I tease her earlobe with my lips, keeping my voice low.

"I know the library's the best spot on campus. Top floor, rarely used reference section. The trick is to stay quiet so no one catches you while you fool around."

She's fucking adorable when her mouth pops open in shock like that. "You've had sex in here?"

"Not yet. Had this bio major ride my fingers while she was on a study break for her finals last year, though." I play with her hair. "Have you?"

"N-no, of course not." Cheeks tinged pink, she clears her throat and packs up her things. "I'm ready to go."

"Mm, good. Meet me on the top floor in five minutes. I'll show you the best spot to finger your..." I scan the tables around us, smirking at the two students doing a poor job of pretending they're not listening. "Pages."

Her wild gaze flies to mine. "Alex!"

God, when she says my name like that all breathy and strained it does things to me. I quell the thrill that shoots through me.

"Just playing around, sweetheart. I've never done any of that. This is my first time here. I'm sorry." I kiss her temple and offer to carry her stuff. She holds on to her tote bag. "I like it when you turn all red like that. You're pretty when you're flustered."

"I—you don't mean that." Her eyes dart around on our way out. "You know all the right things to say. You're good at this. Pretending."

Her voice goes so quiet at the end, I have to strain to hear her while we walk across campus in the direction of the dorms. My lopsided grin falls once the word registers.

"I'm not."

Because I don't think I'm pretending.

I'm not sure when, but sometime in the last week I forgot we were supposed to be faking this. I haven't thought about what happens after her dance. The idea of getting with any other girl is the last thing on my mind, let alone looking at the ones who like to flirt with me.

Maybe it was the moment I saw Lainey in my jersey, or when I first stepped between her and Mike with protectiveness thundering through me, or seeing her light up talking about the book she's reading.

All of these things I might have missed if I wasn't paying attention like I am now.

Hell, maybe this pull toward her has been there since I caught the glimpse of her in the kitchen and it's been dormant until she reawakened it. I can't pinpoint it.

All I know is I want this with her now. I've never allowed myself to get close enough to someone to have a relationship. This isn't the distraction I worried it could be. Not with her.

I like being around her. She's been here all along and I regret that it's taken me so long to become aware of her again.

I'm not willing to let this go. I love hockey, but the way I feel when I'm with her is something special I know I have to chase. To keep.

My gaze slides to study her profile. She remains quiet, maybe as lost in her own thoughts as I am. The cold's turned her nose red. Looking at her makes my heart race and my stomach feel weird in a good way. It's a buzzing energy, like when I score a goal or get a killer assist on the ice.

"Lainey," I rasp.

Her steps falter at my urgent tone. "Are you okay?"

"Yeah. I will be." I snake an arm around her waist. "Come here."

"What are you—?"

The end of her question is muffled by my lips sealing over hers at last. Not her cheek. Not the corner of her mouth.

This isn't an almost-kiss, it's a real one. The kiss I secretly wanted four years ago in her kitchen.

There's nothing fake about the way I claim her mouth, the kiss demanding and hungry. She gives herself over to me so sweetly, fumbling movements following my lead to kiss me back, mouth opening for me when I sweep my tongue against it.

Fuck. Heat sears through me. I've been with a lot of girls. How does a single kiss undo me?

Lainey remains still when we part. Her eyes are shut, her breath coming in sharp little pants that I want to swallow. My hold on her tightens.

One taste isn't enough. I need more of her.

ELEVEN
LAINEY

THE WALK from the library to my dorm is a fevered blur. Alex stops me twice to kiss me again until my knees are weak and my core aches with desire. This frenzied passion only seemed like it existed in my books, but I'm swept up by the inferno building between us. We're both short of breath when we stumble through the lobby of my dorm building.

Alex's fingers slip beneath my sweater on the elevator, seeking skin. Each gasp I draw is thick, my body a live wire that reacts to every touch. I clamp my thighs together when his hot breath ghosts over my throat.

"Do you have a roommate we need to kick out?"

The raw, gritty tone sends a shiver down my spine. I shake my head, concentrating hard to form the words.

"I was supposed to, but she transferred to a different school. Haven't had a replacement."

"Good." His fingers thread through my hair and I arch my body into his when he brings his lips to my neck like he did in the library. The curve of his mouth is like a brand on my skin. "You like that?"

All I'm capable of is a tight whimper that catches in my throat.

The elevator stops on the fourth floor. He takes his time scraping his teeth on my skin even after the doors open.

Peeling away, he snags my hand. "Lead the way."

Thankfully I'm only a few doors from the elevator. I'm too dizzy with want to think straight, let alone walk steadily.

After fumbling for my key at my door, he bats my hand away and unlocks it for me. He captures my waist and herds me inside, lips connecting with the spot beneath my ear before the door swings shut. I gasp at the hard ridge he grinds against my back.

He spins me around to capture my mouth in a sensual kiss that causes another wave of heat in my core. Within moments he plucks my tote bag off my arm, discards his backpack, and kicks off his shoes before nudging me to the bed—all without breaking the kiss.

"Very coordinated," I say.

The sound of his laugh is rich and warm against my cheek. "I've got skills, baby."

Alex kneels at my feet to untie my boots, tapping each leg when he wants me to take them off. The intimate move catches me off guard until he rises to his full height. He removes my glasses with tender care and folds them for me, setting them aside.

Then he gives me another languid kiss. I chase his lips when he pulls away. His amused rumble triggers a sensual twist low in my stomach.

"Don't forget what I said. If you want a kiss," he says in a playful tone. "Just ask, baby."

My cheeks prickle. "I—kissing you is nice."

I've fantasized about it so much in the last week, but my imagination doesn't do Alex Keller justice. The way he kisses and touches me sets my entire body ablaze. I never dreamed I'd actually be kissing him.

Eyes gleaming, he reaches behind his head to tug off his hoodie and t-shirt, baring his sculpted muscles.

"Other parts of me are nice, too."

He takes my hand with a smirk and presses it to his chest, encouraging me to touch him. I lick my lips, skating my palm over the hard planes of his body while he pops the button on my jeans, guiding me to step out of them. His fingertips drag up my thigh as he kisses my throat.

Despite my oversized sweater, I feel like I'm standing naked before him with my legs exposed, as if the rush of desire throbbing in my core is on display. There's no way I'm stopping him, though. Wherever this is going, I want it.

For once I'm going to be like the heroines in my books, in charge of my own story.

With gentle movements, he coaxes me to my bed, crawling over me.

"I want to see all of you," he says against my neck.

His hands delve beneath my sweater again, caressing my body while he maps it with scorching kisses, settling between my legs as he works his way lower.

All of it feels incredible.

Will it still feel this good when he enters me? The stray thought snags my attention.

I've tried it once with a toy I keep hidden in my bottom drawer, then stuck to my usual vibrator on my clit technique because it was *tight*. All the other girls he's used to being with know what they're doing.

As he kisses every inch of skin he exposes, I close my eyes. "I—I've never, um..."

Alex pauses long enough that I crack my eyes open. My breath hitches. He stares up the length of my body with a smoldering gaze, broad shoulders keeping my thighs spread apart to accommodate him.

"Never what, baby?"

He kisses right above my panty line, kneading my hips when my belly concaves. He continues, asking questions as his lips brush a trail along my inner thigh, closer and closer to my aching core that's begging for him.

"Never been tasted?" With each kiss, his eyes flick back to mine, glinting with primal heat. "Never had your sweet pussy touched, stroked, filled until you come so good it makes you want to cry? Never been fucked?"

"All of it," I admit hoarsely.

He studies me for the span of several heartbeats. The weight of it doesn't make me feel self-conscious about being inexperienced. With a burst of courage, I sit up and peel my sweater all the way off, flinging it aside. I ditch my bra next.

"Oh, fuck," he rasps. "Look at me, sweetheart."

I gulp, meeting his piercing eyes again. My face is on fire.

The corner of his mouth lifts, slow and devastating. "I'm going to make you feel so fucking good, baby."

He splays a hand on my stomach and encourages me to lay down. Holding my gaze, he dips his head to mouth at me through my underwear, rumbling in satisfaction when I gasp and squirm.

"I love that I'm the first to see you like this. First to taste you when you come."

A gust of air tears out of him, making my clit throb. He shifts between my legs, eyelids lowering to half mast as he bites back a sexy moan. The bed rocks and I rise up on an elbow to watch him grind against the mattress, fascinated and turned on beyond belief.

"I'm so hard from the thought of being your first. Give me a second to calm down."

"Okay," I stammer.

He chuckles, raking his eyes over me as he reaches down to adjust himself. It's one of the sexiest things I've ever seen. Wonder filters through the pleasurable haze enveloping me. I'm doing that to him?

I don't have long to think about it before he hooks his fingers in my panties and rips them off, no longer going slow to tease me.

"Hold on, sweetheart. To the headboard. Your sheets. My hair." He places a kiss on my folds that makes me tremble. "Hold on tight while I enjoy eating you."

Alex covers my pussy with his mouth and a shocked cry tears out of me at the first long drag of his tongue parting me. He groans, the rough, filthy sound sending a delicious vibration straight to my core.

"Oh!" My spine bows and my fingers have a mind of their own, flying to his head to grip the thick strands of his hair. "Alex, oh my god."

He hums in agreement, large hands molding to my hips to keep me in place. I writhe as he devours me with his mouth, sucking and licking to bring me pleasure I've never imagined.

"Fuck, you're getting so wet," he mutters against my throbbing clit, bringing another new sensation that drives me wild. "That's it, baby. Let me taste you."

The moan that erupts from me is louder than I expect. I'm used to staying quiet, always aware of my surroundings. I've never lost control like this.

His mouth curves in a smug grin against my folds and he massages my hips. "Shh, baby. You're going to let the whole floor know what we're doing. Those sounds are mine. Save them for me while I'm enjoying my meal."

Alex buries his face between my legs and my breath hitches with another strangled cry. Within moments of his skilled ministrations, I'm on the edge.

"I—I think I'm... Oh god, please," I whimper.

He doesn't stop. A rumble vibrates in his throat and he focuses his attention on my clit while I rock against his face in desperate need to chase the perfect friction. The sensations grow more intense, every swipe of his tongue sending me to the brink. My fingers tighten in his hair as my core erupts in a ripple of ecstasy.

"Alex!" I scream.

The orgasm unlike any I've had, deep and intense, going on forever. I ride the waves, chest heaving and body trembling. He strokes my sides and kisses my hip.

"You taste so good when you come on my tongue," he rasps.

His praise filters in and out. I float back to awareness gradually, arching into the delicious aftershocks tingling through me.

Alex watches me, sitting on the edge of the bed. His fingertips trace patterns on my flushed skin. He catches my hand when I reach for the bulge in his pants ready to reciprocate how good he made me feel. I pinch my brows.

Licking my lips, I shift to my knees. My nipples harden at my boldness, sitting in front of him naked. "I want to touch you."

He strokes my hand with his thumb and stares at me with an intent expression I can't decipher. His eyes bounce between mine and he sighs.

"Next time." He tightens his grip to keep me from

pulling away, features strained. "I don't want to push you for something in the heat of the moment, sweetheart. Not more than I already have. Let's take it slow, okay?"

I slide my lips together. "I might be inexperienced, but I know stuff." My books give me a healthy list of fantasies I want to try. Tilting my head, I trace my fingers over my breasts, grasping at the boldness he inspires in me. "I have a vibrator in the drawer over there. You could come in my mouth while I use it on myself."

"Shit. You're killing me," he mutters. "As much as I want nothing more than to have your mouth on my cock, I need to go, baby. I'll be late for practice if I don't go grab my gear now."

Disappointment flares in my chest, but it doesn't last. He shifts closer and caresses my side, drinking me in.

"Just because I have to go doesn't mean you have to stop, though." The tip of his tongue drags over his lower lip. "I want you to use that vibrator to keep playing with yourself. You're going to think of my tongue lapping up every fucking drop from your pussy when you come. Okay?"

Air rushes out of me and my thighs clench. "O-okay."

Alex kisses me deeply, ending it before I'm ready. Then he leaves.

I do what he suggested, pretending he's still the one touching me. But I don't stop at playing by myself until I'm trembling.

Swept up in the lingering daring side he brought out, I record a voice clip of myself when I come with his name on my lips and text it to him. Two hours later, his response makes me smile.

> **Alex**
> Fuck, baby. Fuuuuuuuck.

TWELVE
ALEX

"Someone get that!" Theo shouts from the living room when there's a knock at our door on Friday.

"I've got it," I answer on my way down the steps to the front hall.

Another knock sounds, more timid this time. I open it, finding a gorgeous sight that makes the corners of my mouth pull into a broad grin.

Lainey stands there with her hand raised to knock again. She leaves it hovering for a moment, then adjusts her glasses. My gaze sweeps over her, drinking in the oversized caramel colored sweater that highlights her eyes and her long legs accentuated by black leggings.

The warmth that expands my chest whenever I'm with her is becoming familiar.

Last time I saw her was earlier in the week when I had her spread out on her bed looking fucking perfect before I had to leave for practice.

Her doing, not mine. If it were up to me, I would've prioritized time to see her every day since then. Even with a strenuous practice schedule and our home game yesterday, I've tried to make plans to spend time with her. She keeps shooting me down, swearing she's been way too busy with the final details of her dance preparations for tomorrow night's benefit.

The memory of how I left her—and the insanely hot voice clip she sent of her pleasuring herself while I was playing hockey—ignites the urge to kiss her until she's as off-kilter as I am because of my obsession with her.

Slow, I remind myself. She needs slow.

"Hey, you're a little early. The party won't get going for another hour at least."

"I know." She bites her lip. "It was either show up early or drive myself crazy waiting around. There's nothing else I can do to get ready for tomorrow night's benefit, either. And I couldn't start the next chapter of my current book, because then I wouldn't be at a good stopping point anymore."

An amused hum leaves me. I clasp her wrist and draw her through the door until she steps into me. My head dips to brush my lips against her hair.

"Didn't say I was complaining, sweetheart," I murmur.

"Oh," she breathes unevenly.

"Come on. We can hang out upstairs for a while."

My hand engulfs hers. I tangle our fingers together and lead her to my room.

She hesitates on the threshold with a glance at me, then she steps inside and releases my hand. "So this is the promised land. Alex Keller's bedroom."

I smirk. "It's not anything special."

She peers over her shoulder with a soft, beautiful smile. "I wouldn't say that. It feels like you."

I brace my shoulder against the wall, watching her explore my space. She pauses to look at the Hockey East Rookie of the Year trophy I was honored to receive from last season, then smiles at a photo of Theo and me at training camp from years ago. I scan the room, wondering how she sees it through her eyes.

She points at one of my first hockey trophies from all the way back in youth league. "It's good to see you're proud of all your accomplishments."

"My mom sent that," I explain. "It's, uh. One of my good luck charms."

Her expression falters for a moment, growing distant before she seems to come back to herself. "That's really sweet."

She moves on to the shelf above my desk where I keep my prized collection of signed pucks. My tongue swipes across my lower lip and I rub at the glowing sensation expanding in my chest.

I really want to kiss her again. Fuck, I want to do so much more than that, too. But I told her we'd take this slow. Otherwise, I'll have trouble controlling myself when it comes to her.

I already stripped her naked and buried my face between her legs after one addictive kiss. If I hadn't stopped myself when she reached for my cock, I would've fucked her, no question.

This isn't a hookup. I'm going to do this differently with her.

She deserves to be treated right. I want to go slow at her pace so she's comfortable.

"You look good in this picture." Her shy, warm tone does things to me.

I can't resist any longer. Pressing off the wall, I close the distance between us, wrapping my arms around her from behind. Lifting her chin, I capture her mouth in a languid kiss.

After a moment, I maneuver us to the bed. I drop down to sit on the edge, pulling her with me so she lands with a knee on either side of my lap.

She breaks away to slip off her glasses, reaching for

the nightstand. I help since I have a longer reach, setting them safely out of the way.

"That's better," she says.

"No, this is better." I pull her back in and slant my lips over hers, mumbling against her mouth. "Much better."

She hums, winding her arms around my shoulders. My hands roam down her sides, then beneath her sweater to grasp her waist. I love the way each touch makes her kiss me more urgently. She's so responsive, straining against me while soft noises of pleasure escape her.

If she keeps grinding on me like that, I'm going to flip her over, pin her to the bed, and make her scream my name again with my cock filling her up.

Shit. As much as I want to tear her clothes off and explore every inch of her, I have to take this at a steady pace.

What counts as slow? The concept has been lost to me.

I speak against her plush lips. "Do you know how badly I want to spread you out on this bed?" Her breath hitches. I trail my mouth to find her ear. "All I can think about is how much I want to taste you again. I want to spend hours with my tongue inside your pussy."

Lainey shudders, hips bucking. My fingers dig into her hips and a rumble builds in my chest.

"Please," she whimpers, seeking me out for another heady kiss.

I give her what she needs for a moment, then pull back. "We're not alone and the walls are thinner in this old house than they are in the dorms. Can you be quiet?"

She nods. "I don't care. Please touch me. Do anything to me, Alex."

I rake my teeth across my lower lip and release a ragged breath. "God, baby. You're driving me crazy with all those pretty sounds you make."

Sliding my hand from her hip to her ass, I tease my fingers between her legs. She arches back, giving me better access. I smirk at the damp spot on her leggings from just grinding on my erection. Each graze of my fingertips causes her to shiver.

She tips her head back, baring her throat to me. I lean forward and pepper it with open-mouthed kisses.

I stretch out against the mattress on my back, encouraging her to come with me while she straddles me. She braces her hands on my shoulders.

Finding the waistband of her leggings, I push them down to expose her ass. She bites her lip, eyelashes fluttering from the cool air hitting her flushed skin. I trace patterns across her ass with my fingertips, then pet her through her panties until she presses back in a silent plea for more.

With a deft move, I tug her underwear aside and glide two fingers through her slick folds. She trembles, tiny cries and moans catching in her throat the longer I tease her.

"So wet for me. Do you want more?"

"Yes."

My fingers circle her hole a few times to get her ready before I sink one inside. She's tight, but her pussy is dripping so much that it helps ease the way. The reactions flickering across her features are beautiful. I want more of them, working my finger deeper and curling it.

"Oh!" Her hands scrabble at my shirt.

I give her hip a squeeze with my other hand. "Keep rocking your hips, baby. Use me to make your clit feel good while I fuck you with my fingers."

Blonde hair swings down to create a curtain around her face. I tuck it behind her ear to have an unobstructed view of her face. She begins to move her hips, using the bulging erection in my jeans for friction. I allow her to set the pace, matching it with my finger.

It's not long before her flush deepens and her chest

heaves with each breath. I add a second finger, savoring the feeling of her stretched around both of them. She finds a rhythm of rocking her hips to give her clit pressure and meet each thrust of my fingers inside her.

"Are you going to rub against me until you come all over my fingers?" I rasp.

"Oh my god." She moans. "Yes. It feels so—"

She breaks off and the corners of my mouth lift in satisfaction. "That's it. Don't stop, Lainey."

When her hips falter and she clenches on my fingers, a loud moan tears from her. I cover her mouth with my free hand to keep anyone else from hearing her come undone for me. I keep playing with her while she rides out her orgasm, murmuring praise to her.

I could spend the rest of the night watching her face while I make her come over and over.

But her brother is right downstairs. And probably half of Heston's campus by now for the party.

Pulling my fingers free, I sit up and fix her leggings. She keeps her hands to herself in her lap, plucking at the hem of her sweater. Her eyes are dazed and her lips pull into a soft smile to match mine.

I curl an arm around her and show off my glistening fingers. "This will have to tide me over until the next time I can enjoy my new favorite meal."

With a smirk at her surprise, I lick them clean,

groaning when lust flares in her gaze. She tugs at my wrist, then cups my jaw before leaning in to kiss me.

Reluctantly, I stop her long before I'm ready to end it. My erection shows no signs of flagging, even though I need it to calm down. Shit, maybe I'll have to rub one out really quick to take the edge off.

"Do you need anything or want to freshen up?" I sigh. "The bathroom's a shared one, though. Really wishing I had the captain's room so I had my own private one."

She shakes her head, granting me a sly look that I like on her. "I'll be okay. I'm pretty sure you took care of all that clean up."

Chuckling, I grab her beneath her thighs and shoot to my feet, enjoying the way she holds on tight with a little yelp. After a quick peck, I set her down.

"Where are you going?"

She hovers by the bed. Her playfulness disappears, becoming uncertain.

I'm at a loss for how to explain for a moment, gesturing at my rock hard dick. "I was planning on jerking off in the bathroom before we go downstairs."

Confusion twists her features. "What? Why?"

I drag a hand through my hair, probably messing it up even more than she already has from gripping it while we made out.

"I don't want to push you for something you're not ready—"

"Alex." She closes the small distance I put between us and rests a hand on my chest. "I'm an adult and fully capable of consenting to touch your dick."

Her matter of fact response makes me chuckle. She drags her hand down to rub my cock through my jeans, causing my laughter to transform into a choked back groan.

"You're killing me."

"I think you like it," she counters.

"Definitely."

I'm grinning when I kiss her.

The door swings open a few moments later. I move instinctively, whipping us around so whoever the hell thought it was a good idea to barge into my room without knocking doesn't see my girl like this. Her stunning, hazy eyes when she comes undone are for me and me alone.

I crane my neck, using my body as a shield. One of the rookies leans his head in.

"Yo, you're missing—oh, shit. Sorry," Easton trails off once he sees my glare. "Theo sent me on a mission to find you, but you're busy. I'll just..."

"Close the fucking door on your way out," I say.

"Yup, definitely doing that. Hi Lainey."

She giggles. "Hi Easton."

"I'll be guarding the pizza rolls until you come down to the party."

"You have five seconds to get out of here, Blake," I warn.

"Gone, I'm gone," he promises through the crack in the door. "Poof. Where did E go? He disappeared. Wow, magic."

Lainey buries her face in my chest to stifle her laughter at his antics.

Keeping her wrapped in my arms, I collapse on the bed. "Give me a minute to calm down."

"That's no fun." She props her chin on my chest. "I'd rather stay up here with you than go down to the party."

A glint of mischief dances in her eyes. It's a sexy as fuck look on her, like my own corrupt little librarian.

My cock strains with a pulse of heat as she bites her lip and works a hand between us to stroke me again.

"Fuck, baby," I rasp.

She studies me intently. "Is that okay?"

Christ. Her earnestness to learn how to touch me and what I like is so damn hot.

My eyes fall shut with a groan and I nod. "Yes."

"Can I see it?"

Her beautiful brown eyes bounce between mine

when my eyes fly open. A silent question passes between us that she seems to understand without me voicing it. She gives my cock a squeeze, breaking the last of my resolve to keep our clothes on this time.

Keeping my gaze locked with hers, I shift her off me and pop the button on my jeans. I take her hand and slide it inside my pants, releasing a rough exhale when she works her way past the elastic waistband on my boxers and brushes her fingers against skin. She breaks our stare, watching me lower my zipper and jerk my clothes down.

Her eyes widen. "It looks even bigger than it felt through your clothes."

Another chuckle falls from my lips and pride stirs in my chest. Out of all the girls that have been in my bed, nothing they've said compares to how good it feels for her to tell me my dick is big. I cover her hand with mine, both of us working together to stroke it.

"Like that," I murmur as pleasure courses through my veins.

My hand falls away and she takes over. Then she places a sweet, gentle kiss on my cheek before sliding off the bed to kneel beside it.

"Sit up," she says.

My cock is so hard it leaves me lightheaded when I do what she wants. I fist my hands in the blanket to keep from turning into a caveman while she continues her exploration, fingers wrapped around my length while she brings her mouth to the head to give it a curious lick.

"Lainey," I push out. "You don't have to—oh, *fuck!*"

Her lips close around my cock. My chest heaves and my grip turns rigid on the blanket to keep myself in check. I don't even care that her technique is a little clumsy. Her mouth is my new wet, hot fucking heaven.

I'm not going to last long, too turned on to hold out for more.

She tries to swallow my cock whole, making a strangled noise when she's taken me halfway. She pulls back to catch her breath, cheeks tinged pink.

"Easy, baby," I encourage. "Don't push yourself."

My heartbeat stutters when she peers up at me with those big brown eyes and swipes her tongue over the tip. I hold her gaze, mouth parted while I grip the base of my shaft to help her.

Watching her work me with her mouth while I stroke myself is driving me crazy. This is hotter than anything I've ever experienced.

Her mouth feels too damn good on me. It takes everything in me to slow my hand down once I'm close.

"I'm going to come," I warn.

She doesn't release me, taking my length another inch deeper with the sexiest little moan I've ever heard.

"Sweetheart, seriously, if you don't..."

I try to explain that if she doesn't stop, she's getting a mouthful of come, but I can't form the right words. She moans again, giving my cock a hard suck that almost sends me over the edge.

"You want to taste my come? Want it to fill your mouth?"

She manages an eager nod. Fuck, I want to finish in her mouth.

My head tips forward as my orgasm punches the air from my lungs. I sink my fingers into her hair with a curse, my come flooding her mouth.

She goes still, both of us panting. Then she swallows, and I feel like I could come again right away from how incredible it feels.

Running my fingers through her hair, I lean back, gaze roaming over her. I hope I didn't hurt her.

"Are you okay?"

"Yeah, I'm great," she assures me while I tuck myself back in my boxers.

A streak of my come dribbles down her face from the corner of her mouth. I swipe it up with my thumb, eyes hooding as she turns to lick it up. My heart won't stop racing, the damn thing beating hard enough I'm surprised we both can't hear it.

"Come up here."

Lainey giggles when I tug her from the floor into my embrace. Her cute laughter is silenced when my mouth collides with hers.

My arms tighten around her as I kiss her harder. I don't want to move from this spot or leave this room.

THIRTEEN
LAINEY

Posing as Alex's fake girlfriend isn't difficult, like I believed it would be. It's the complete opposite, so easy that it should worry me that I'm having trouble recognizing what's fake and what's something more since he first kissed me earlier this week. I could understand the kiss on campus while he walked me back from the library, but everything else we've done? I'm not sure what it means.

It's not like there was anyone to watch us after we got back to my dorm, or when he led me upstairs tonight. There wasn't any reason to put on an act behind closed doors.

All I know is that I really like what we're doing.

Another surprise is how quickly I've grown used to

being around the hockey guys in a short span of time. They're not so bad.

I'm actually having a good time tonight after we finally made it down to the party.

Looking my brother in the eye after giving his best friend a blowjob is one of the last things I want to do. He stared at me, then at Alex, well aware that we were alone together in his bedroom for over an hour. My lips were still slightly swollen, but I lifted my chin rather than give in to the urge to run away. I don't regret any of it.

Theo narrowed his eyes, but kept his mouth shut.

After we've made the rounds to say hi to people Alex knows, he drops a kiss on my temple and runs back upstairs to his room to get his phone off the charger, leaving me with my brother and one of the freshmen players in the kitchen.

"I'm telling you, pizza rolls with ranch are superior," I argue with Easton while Theo gets a tray of them out of the oven.

"This is ketchup slander," he declares. "It goes on everything."

My nose wrinkles at the thought of ketchup on pizza rolls. He grabs one of the mini lava pockets and tosses it between his hands with a pained expression.

"You're an idiot." Theo snorts. "At least wait until they cool off. You trying to burn your tongue off?"

"But I'm hungry." Easton blows on the roll before shoving it in his mouth while it's still too hot based on the way his entire body shuffles around.

Theo shoots me a long suffering look. "Sometimes I think I miss when I lived at home. I actually got to eat, for one."

"Can you get the—"

"I'm on it." Theo rummages in the refrigerator and sets the ranch on the counter.

"You're team ranch, too?" Easton's expression crumples as if his teammate has betrayed him in the worst way. "Nah, bro. How are you gonna do me like that?"

"Because it tastes better," Theo says.

I laugh, then jolt when strong arms circle me from behind, tugging me against a firm body. Alex presses a smile against my cheek.

"Lainey."

"What?"

"Hi." He kisses my jawline when an amused noise escapes me and his arms cinch tighter. "What are you doing?"

I catch my brother's eye roll and exasperated smirk as he turns his back on us.

"Making pizza rolls." I shiver, licking my lips when

Alex plays with the hem of my sweater. A sizzle of heat races through me, reminding me of what we did in his room. "They're secret, though. There isn't enough for everyone here."

He hums. "Is that why you've got Higgins posted up in the hallway to keep people out of here?"

The huge defensive player has an intimidating permanent scowl. I was low-key afraid of him before Alex introduced his teammates at the last party. Theo insisted I had to be the one to ask Higgins if he'd redirect people from the kitchen while we worked on our secret snack project. It was the first time his scowl melted when he agreed gruffly.

"He's being rewarded for his efforts," Easton interjects as he piles steaming snacks in his hand. "Fuck, these are so hot still."

It feels like our own private party when the four of us crowd around the island. Theo pretends to gag while Alex feeds me pizza rolls. Easton still insists he's team ketchup. I'm enjoying the bubble we've created, feeling a sense of fitting in from the world I kept myself separate from for so long.

After our snack, Alex takes my hand and we go to the living room. It feels so natural now to hold his hand or lean against his side with his arm around me while we hang out with people he knows.

He talks up my benefit to anyone who will listen. It's enough to make me blush. Each time he looks at me, there's wonder in his handsome green eyes. I'm looking forward to seeing him in a suit again for the dance tomorrow night.

I put a hand on his arm while he's having a conversation about Heston's next game. "I'll be back. I need a drink."

"Want me to come with you?" He laces our fingers together to keep me by his side.

I bite my lip to hold back the smile fighting to break free. "I'll be two minutes."

He kisses my hand. "Miss you already."

"You're cheesy," I say.

He winks. I head to the kitchen with my insides fluttering.

"Hey!" The familiar bubbly voice snags my attention.

I offer a shy smile to Candace, the sorority girl I first met at the Heston U vs UConn hockey game.

"Please, please tell me you're going to get ready with us tomorrow?" She holds her hands in front of her like a prayer. "I'm dying to do your makeup. I just got this great winter palette with shades that would look so good on you."

This isn't the first time she's asked since we met two

weeks ago. I've given excuses because I didn't think she'd want to hang out, but she hasn't dropped it.

We've been texting since I gave her my number. I've continued adding to the list of book recommendations I gave her when she came to the bookstore. Part of me wonders if I'm annoying her by sending so many, but she responds with so much enthusiastic interest when I message her with another book I think she might want to try that it sets me at ease.

"Okay, but only if you don't mind doing me first because I'll need to leave early for the banquet hall to make sure the vendors have everything they need."

Candace claps in excitement. "Yay! Oh, I finished the first book on the list. It was so good, girl. I'm hooked. Is the next one available at the bookshop?"

My eyes widen. "You liked it?"

"*Loved* it." She fans herself while she gushes. "Oh my god, I was swooning. Then I needed to call my boyfriend when things got spicy."

My face flushes, but I nod in understanding. "We have the whole series in stock."

Someone in another room calls her name. She squeezes my shoulder.

"Text me tomorrow. You can come over as early as you want. I'm doing a full self-care day before the event."

"Okay."

I'm relieved that she gave me a time frame so I don't get stuck wondering when to go there. It's nice to have another friend besides Maya to talk to about books I've read. Alex doesn't count since he's been my new mental image for all the book boyfriends I read. I find myself looking forward to tomorrow, ready to enjoy myself after all my hard work on the dance.

Pouring myself a drink, I head back toward Alex with a tiny smile breaking free. I stop just outside the room when I hear something that turns my insides to stone.

"Keller, what's the deal with you and Brainy? Why are you even with that nerd?"

Every muscle in my body stiffens and my throat closes. It's Mike and his asshole friends on the football team.

I was so swept up in what's happening with Alex that I forgot why he wanted to pretend with me in the first place.

"What makes you think I have to explain myself to you?" Alex's usual easygoing tone takes on a hard edge. "I'm with her, end of story."

My heart clenches. I want to believe he means that, more than I've ever wanted anything in my life. When he kissed me, I allowed myself to think two total opposites like us could work because the way I feel when I'm with him is so right.

But it's not real, is it?

We agreed to play this act for two weeks and that's exactly what he's doing—making it appear like he's really my boyfriend.

"I'm asking you straight up," Mike continues. "You can have any girl you want. Why her—unless she fucks like a puck bunny? Oh shit, it is, isn't it? Don't deny it, it's written all over your face. Does she let go of that uptight, bitchy attitude when she's on her knees taking cock in her mouth?"

Puck bunny. The term makes my stomach sink. How could I forget this is how athletes talk about the women they sleep with?

Shaking my head, I abandon my drink on the nearest flat surface. I don't need to stick around for this. There's a shout, followed by a commotion. I don't stop to find out what it's about while I slip through the front door.

The first thought that cuts through the buzz over-taking my mind questions if that's how Alex thinks of this thing between us, too. Before he decided to become my fake boyfriend his reputation for hookups was rampant across campus. Am I a puck bunny to him? Or maybe I'm not enough like one, too inexperienced to appeal to him.

Alex can get with any girl. So why would he want me?

I was kidding myself believing I fit in here. I don't. I never will.

A thick lump clogs my throat. I swallow it, trying to get my strained breathing under control.

Embarrassment rakes down my spine. I felt so sexy and confident with him. Now those intimate moments are tarnished by what I overheard.

Nerds and jocks don't belong together. The divide will always exist between us.

My eyes itch and sting on my walk through town. It's not because of the winter air.

Our two weeks of faking our relationship are up. Time to get back to reality.

FOURTEEN
ALEX

ONE MINUTE, I'm enjoying the party, waiting for Lainey to come back, then the next minute, I'm overcome by anger. My cup drops from my hand and spills on my shoes when I hear that idiot running his mouth. A dangerous, icy chill spreads through me.

Mike doesn't finish his next sentence before my fist smashes into his jaw with so much force he stumbles back. I want to break every bone in his body for what he said about Lainey.

He still thinks he has any right to challenge me over my girl?

Fuck no.

I should've laid him out like this the first time I caught him messing with Lainey on the quad.

Two of my boys flank me as my chest heaves, fury burning in my veins.

"Shut your goddamn mouth, Rivers," I grit out. "You're out of fucking line."

Clenching my jaw, I grip the collar of his Heston U hoodie. The expression on his face is fucking ugly. It's the look of a loser who would never deserve someone like her.

He'll never have her, either. She's mine. Even if she wasn't, I wouldn't let him near her.

With a furious yell, I punch him again. I never lose control of myself, not on the ice or off it.

I'll fucking kill him for what he said. Who the hell does he think he is? He has no right to say that shit about her. No one does.

If I haven't made that crystal fucking clear, now it should be.

Theo grabs my arm when I pull it back for another hit and two other guys help him pull me off. Mike's face is swollen and red, the corner of his mouth bleeding.

"As much as I'm enjoying watching you pound his ass, that's enough. I'm not letting you risk your future. Lainey wouldn't want that either." Theo squeezes my shoulder in support and pats it when I drop my arm in acceptance. He glares at Mike. "Get the fuck out. You'd better hope we never hear you talking shit about my sister ever again."

I rake a hand through my hair, picturing my girl's sweet smile to calm me down.

Shit. Where is she? I scan the party, moving from room to room while the guys take care of kicking that dickhead Rivers and his friends out.

"Hey." I snag Easton by the arm. "Where's Lainey?"

He shakes his head. "Haven't seen her, man. She was in the kitchen right before the fight broke out, but she's gone now."

"Fuck." I blow out a breath.

I send her a text to check on her, but she doesn't respond. Agitated worry creates a weight in my stomach. Raking a hand through my hair, I step out on the porch to call her. The first try rings once before it drops. Frowning, I call her back. This time it goes right to voicemail.

Things were so perfect upstairs in my room when it was just the two of us. I wish we were back there now.

Theo's sprawled in the cushy chair in the corner with a girl perched on the arm rest when I come back inside.

"Can you call Lainey? I'm only getting her voicemail."

"She left?"

"Yeah, I can't find her. Easton said she's gone."

He mutters to himself, then digs his phone from his pocket, smirking at the girl he's flirting with when the movement jostles her. "Don't worry. She hates too much attention. She probably ran home because she's embarrassed. It's what she does when she wants to shut out the world."

I ball my fist and grip my phone harder when he shakes his head. "I'll go find her."

If she heard Mike and me fighting, it must have upset her. I hate the thought of that asshole making her cry. I clench my jaw and start for the door.

"She's fine," Theo calls after me.

I frown. "You're seriously not worried about her?"

He shrugs. "Just let her be for tonight. If you get in her face when she wants to be left alone, it only makes it ten times worse. Trust me. She likes to work shit out on her own."

The last thing I want to do is stress her out more or hurt her feelings worse.

Theo levels me with a knowing look. He can read me better than anyone. I trust him. Even though everything in me wants to track her down and hold her.

I lift my hands. "Fine. I'll wait until tomorrow and give her time to herself. But first thing in the morning, I'm going to find her and make sure she's okay."

"You do you, man."

"I will."

Not in the mood to party without my girl, I head upstairs. She still won't answer when I try to call again. Sighing, I start sending texts. I have no idea if she's reading them or not, but they're the only thing keeping me from going out of my mind.

> **Alex**
> I'm sorry about tonight, sweetheart.

> **Alex**
> You freaked me out when you left by yourself. Are you okay?

> **Alex**
> Talk to me. Please?

> **Alex**
> If you're mad about me punching Mike, he deserved it. I won't let anyone say anything like that about you. He's a fucking douchebag.

> **Alex**
> What do you want for breakfast? I'm coming over first thing in the morning. 🖤

The urge to go after her doesn't leave me all night. I toss and turn, waking up more than once to send her another message when a new important thought pops into my head.

In the morning, I stare blearily at the event reminder on my phone I set two weeks ago for Lainey's benefit dance tonight.

I've forgotten all about the deal I proposed right around the minute I kissed her. We're long past faking it now.

FIFTEEN
LAINEY

My phone remains off. I'm not looking forward to turning it back on.

Ignoring the world, I curl up with Hammy behind the bar in the large cupboard Dad sacrificed storage space for in order to give the dog a comfy bed and a place to chill out. It's a slow night, thankfully. Not many people are around to witness my bitter tears over Alex.

What we have is fake. It was his idea out of some bullshit sense of pity to protect me. He's not mine and after tonight, our deal is off. He'll go back to ignoring my existence. Back to being a player.

I was wrong.

No, I was *right*.

Hockey players are all the same.

I never should have forgotten it because I hate

facing the truth over and over. They're unreliable and all they do is mess up my life and let me down or leave me behind.

Hammy's tail thumps and he presses his full body against me, wiggling to get closer as if he weighs twenty pounds instead of eighty. I hide a sniffle into his neck. With the help of the dog demanding all the attention I'm willing to give, the tightness in my chest loosens enough for me to breathe easier.

The world doesn't exist to me for a while. I'm perfectly content for it to continue like that, until someone interrupts my pity party.

"What's wrong?" Dad braces an arm on the counter, bending down to peer at me and the dog.

"Nothing," I mumble.

"Come on. I know you like to crawl in there with Hammy when something upsets you. What happened?"

When I take too long to answer, he sighs and gives me space, ambling around behind the bar. He cleans glassware and serves the few patrons perched on stools.

Huffing, I stroke Hammy's soft coat. "Like you care."

"What's that, sweetie?"

A lump forms in my throat. I climb out of the hiding spot and glare at the photos on the wall. My embarrassment and pain rise to the surface once more.

"Dad."

He freezes at the rawness in my tone. I wave a hand at the walls when I have his undivided attention for once. This has been a long time coming. I'm done holding it in and accepting something that's always bothered me.

"We both know that you only care about one of your kids. It's clear to see on the walls."

His bewildered expression only makes this hurt more. I don't care that the customers nearest to the bar get front row seats while I open up old wounds that never truly healed. He reaches for me but I stumble backwards.

"You only put Theo's photos up," I say tightly. "His games. Winning trophies. When he got recruited to Heston, you were so happy. But I got my early acceptance first. I work so hard hoping someone will see me, but I'm invisible, even to my own family."

The end of my sentence comes out garbled as I choke the words out through a sob. Hammy whines at my side, pressing his weight into me to ease my distress.

"Theo and hockey are the only things you care about," I push out. "You didn't even care about mom's affair right in front of you. Or that she left us. How can you act like nothing's wrong with that when you go to Theo's games with her and her new husband?"

All of this has been bottled up inside me for so long that it's agonizing to spill out at last.

Dad's preference for Theo, Mom flaunting her cheating and remarriage, Theo being the star athlete everyone knows on campus—all of those are reasons why I couldn't bear to go to hockey games anymore and wanted to stay far away from everything that hurt me. No one asked me why I stopped, or cared about what interests me.

The fresh anguish of hoping for more with Alex after he was the only person to ever look at me and see me for who I am collides with the old, scabbed over wound of my family history. I don't want to be the girl stuck in my brother's shadow anymore.

Dad gives me a stricken look. "Lainey." He drops the bar rag and strides over to me, crushing me in a hug. "No. No, you're not, sweetie. I'm so proud of you. I always have been."

My throat stings. "Then why do you only put Theo in here?"

"You're such a shy girl, I never thought you wanted the attention," he says hoarsely. "You hated it when we'd go out to dinner for your birthday and had them sing when they brought the cake. I'm so sorry. I love you, sweetie. Of course I love you."

Fresh tears spill down my cheeks because I've never

been able to hold it together when my dad gets choked up. He rubs my arms, his expression contorted with guilt.

The fierce hug is exactly what I needed. It's full of his love, chasing away my doubts and the resentments that have pricked my heart for years.

"I'm sorry," I whisper.

"You're sorry? What—why are you apologizing? You have nothing to be sorry for. It's me, I'm the one who needs to be sorry for ever making my baby girl think you're not important to me."

"I don't know. I just am. For not telling you how I felt?"

His laugh is thick and wet, clogging in his throat. "Okay. What would make it feel better? Do you want me to hang your dean's list letters? I keep them all, you know."

"No, it's okay," I whisper.

Despite not wanting to be the invisible girl anymore, the family drama show we're putting on for the rest of the bar has reached the small limit of attention I can handle. I do my best to ignore the uncomfortable sensation of being watched.

"We can talk about it later."

"I promise to do better," he says gruffly. "And you

should talk to your mom about this, too. When you're ready."

I nod and he kisses the top of my head. With one last one-armed bear hug, he shuffles down the bar and ducks into his office.

Sniffling, I swipe my tear-stained cheeks. An older patron seated at the bar passes the pile of cocktail napkins to me. I mutter a thanks, bowing my head.

Dad comes back out with a picture frame and a hammer.

"Dad?" My eyes widen when he yanks down a banner with a list of Heston U hockey players that went on to play in the NHL with their signatures on it. "What are you doing?"

"Place of honor," he explains. "I'm proud as hell of everything you do. Haven't stopped being proud of you since the day you were born. You're way smarter than me or your brother. Anyone who doesn't see every amazing thing about you is a fucking idiot in my book."

When he steps back from hammering the new frame on the wall, I roll my lips between my teeth. It's not my early acceptance letter or any of my official achievements. It's a photo of us at the Heston Lake Ice Rink. I remember how excited I was when he got me and Theo our first pair of ice skates. In the photo, Dad holds my hand and beams at the camera while I concentrate.

A warm glow expands in my chest. It's a balm for the parts of me that shouldered the hurt for years.

"Thanks, Dad. I've got to go." I kiss his cheek. "Tomorrow is a big day."

He nods, scrubbing a hand over his face to regain his composure. "The catering delivery will be ready to go for the end of the night snack bar."

I bite my lip. Booking The Landmark for an order of wings and fries was a last minute addition suggested by Alex.

"Thank you. Oh, and Dad?"

"Yes?"

I give him a shaky smile. "I love you, too."

Leaving the bar, a weight rises off my shoulders. Tonight sucked, but a positive came out of it. Finding the conviction to confront my dad never would've happened if Alex didn't come along and interrupt my world two weeks ago.

From now on, I'm done being invisible. And the next time I see Mike River, I'm telling him to his face what a dick he is.

SIXTEEN
ALEX

Lainey and Theo's dad greets me when I arrive at their house early in the morning with coffee and donuts from Clocktower Brew House.

"Morning, Alex. Are you looking for Theo?" he asks.

It almost feels as though I'm living two lives, my past self who befriended Theo colliding with my present self who fell for his sister.

"I'm here for Lainey."

"Lainey?" His brow furrows.

My chest grows tight and my stomach twists with nerves. "She's—we've started—" I've never had a meet the parents moment since Lainey's my first real girl-friend. It's weirdly intimidating and I'm not sure what to say. "I'm her boyfriend."

"Oh. I didn't know she was dating."

He sizes me up, making the nerves worse. I've known him for years, yet I've never questioned what he thinks of me more than I am right now. My palms grow hot and clammy.

"Hockey keeps you pretty busy, doesn't it?"

"Yes, but she's important to me." The truth pierces my drumming heart. "Really important. I only want to make her happy."

Finally, Mr. Boucher nods. "I'm glad to hear that. You're a good kid, Alex."

Tension bleeds from my shoulders. "Thanks, sir. Is she home?"

He shakes his head. "You missed her by about twenty minutes. She left."

"Oh, uh. Right. Okay." I gesture with the bag of donuts in place of a wave, planning to check her dorm next.

It's not a long trip to campus, but my impatience to see her makes every minute drag. A group of chatty girls heading out of her building with yoga mats block the way when I get there. The last one holds the door for me and I rush inside.

The elevator takes forever, so I find the stairs instead. Relief hits me when I finally reach her room. I juggle the coffee and donuts to knock. When there isn't an answer, I rap my knuckles against the door harder.

Her neighbor across the hall comes out, eyeing me up and down. I clear my throat.

"Sorry if I woke you up."

"You didn't, but you are knocking loudly."

"Have you seen Lainey?"

"Is that her name? She always keeps to herself." She shrugs. "I haven't seen her since yesterday."

Damn it. "Okay, thanks."

If she's not home or in her dorm, she has to be over at the banquet hall getting things ready for tonight. I try calling her again on my way over, still getting her voicemail.

The banquet hall crawls with people. A student sets up DJ equipment while a woman unloads books from a rolling wagon cart on the tables dotted around the room. I don't spot Lainey anywhere.

I go to the guy moving speakers into place at the DJ booth.

"Hey, hand me that cable—yeah, the extension," he says. "Thanks."

"Sure. Is Lainey around?"

"She was." He scans the room. "She's been pretty busy coming and going to direct the other vendors for deliveries."

My shoulders slump. "Thanks."

I wander around without any luck. Before I leave, I give a hand by setting up more tables and help the woman who introduces herself as Mr. Derby's daughter pick up more books from the back room of their store. In all the time I hang around hoping to see her, she's not there.

The text notification on my phone makes me suck in a sharp breath on my way out of the building. Frustration bubbles back to life when it's the wrong Boucher.

> **Theo**
> Are you coming to practice? You're cutting it close. None of the guys want to skate suicides because you're late.

> **Alex**
> No. I'm looking for Lainey.

> **Theo**
> Coach will be pissed if you blow it off.

> **Alex**
> Cover for me.

It's a first for me. I've never missed a game or practice. Injured or sick, I've always wanted to be on the ice.

I'll make up for skipping it later.

It's late in the day by the time I've run all over campus trying to catch her. The coffee I picked up this morning went cold hours ago and I ended up eating both donuts, too busy to stop for anything more substantial while I trying to track her down.

I know eventually I'll be able to find her at the dance, but I didn't plan on waiting that long. At this point, that might be my only choice because I keep missing her and she still won't answer my calls.

Theo might be my best friend and one of the teammates I trust the most, but he was wrong about his sister. I think I messed up by listening to him instead of following what my gut wanted me to do.

If I had gone after her like I wanted last night, I wouldn't have this growing sense of dread that she could slip through my fingers.

Two weeks ago I had no idea what truly caring for someone else felt like. Now that I have it with her, I don't want to let it go or lose it.

Sighing, I scrub a hand over my face. I have to fix this.

The kind of guys she reads about in her romance books wouldn't have fucked up like I have. My brows furrow when I think about what I respected about the cowboy in the book we both read. He knew what he wanted and he didn't let anything get in the way of that.

I'm going to do right by her like he would. Do the right things. Say the right things. Pay attention to her and understand how to keep her happy. Because that's what makes me happy.

Actually, no. Fuck that.

I'm going to be *better* than anyone made up for a story because Lainey is my girl, and I'll be damned if I don't show her that when I should've been there for her.

First plan of action: buy her flowers. Then I need to stop back at the house for my suit.

I'm going to get my girl.

SEVENTEEN
LAINEY

THE TRANSFORMATION in the banquet room for the evening takes my breath away. It's amazing to see it all come together. The book arch at the entrance to the event came out amazing, and giddiness bolts through me at the line of people waiting outside for the doors to open.

Heston's student body showed up for our town's bookshop in a way I couldn't have dreamed when I first decided to do this event. Tickets sold out and I heard from Candace earlier as she applied my makeup that people were looking for any available tickets on the local student-run Facebook group. Rather than make any kind of speech, I opted to post a thank you sign by the ticket check in with all the words I'd be too nervous to say.

I smooth the elegant tiered fabric of my black gown, waiting for the event to begin. Everything is set. If I flit around the room to check on stuff again, the DJ I booked from Heston's Music & Arts department will make good on his joking threat to glue my feet to the floor.

This is the first time I've slowed down all day and it's hitting me that I pulled this off. Not only did ticket sales raise a lot, the college has matched my donation to keep Derby Bookshop in business.

Alex was the first person I wanted to tell when I opened the letter in my mailbox on my way out.

Once I bit the bullet and turned my phone on this morning, I ignored the missed calls and texts from him, only allowing myself one moment for my heart to twinge. The first thing I did was put his texts on mute and silence his calls before burying what happened in the back of my mind.

My whirlwind schedule has kept me busy all day, holding thoughts of him at bay. I'm glad Candace invited me to get ready with her and her friends to take my mind off the anxious thoughts doomscrolling in my head once I stop focusing on the spinning plates keeping me distracted.

I startle when music spills through the room. The fog machines in front of the DJ booth add to the magical purple lighting. I give him a sheepish wave. It's time to let everyone in.

Poking my head through the arch of floating books and their pages, I give the ticket table volunteers a thumbs up. I hang back once people start to enter the room, rolling my lips between my teeth when their expressions fill with excitement.

Some people go to the wall I set up showcasing Derby Bookshop's history with photos Mr. Derby gave me and older ones I pulled from the library. Others find seats at the tables, taking photos of the book stack centerpieces. It's not long before someone discovers the photo booth set up with a fairytale background and a variety of crowns.

After twenty minutes, people are still entering in a steady stream, the room filling. For the first time ever, I'm not doing everything I can to avoid a crowd.

"Hey, girl!" Candace arrives with her sorority sisters. All of them look gorgeous. She leans in to kiss both my cheeks. "Oh my god, this looks so amazing. You did all this?"

I shrug. "A lot of vendors donated their services."

"You did such a great job organizing this. We're hitting up the photo booth first. You'll do it with us, right?"

"In a little bit. Enjoy yourselves tonight."

Candace holds up her arms and does a shimmying dance with her hips. "You know it. Where's your man?"

"Oh." I twist my fingers, the elbow-length gloves suddenly feeling silly and too hot. "I don't know. He's—"

"Late, but I promise I have a good excuse."

I spin around, gaping at Alex. He's here. He still came.

Shock arrows through me. I didn't expect him to come after last night. I thought things were over.

His eyes lock on me, his handsome features shifting from relief to awe as he takes in my gown. "Hi, sweetheart."

The devastating smile only adds to how good he looks in his suit.

"Hi," I breathe.

"Well?" Candace prompts. I forgot she was there. "What's the excuse for being late to your sweet girlfriend's big event?"

Alex holds up a beautiful bouquet of flowers. "The two florist shops in town couldn't take walk-ins, so I had to take a little road trip. Here, these are for you."

"No one's ever given me flowers." It's the first thing I blurt while admiring the mix of roses and sprigs of evergreen. My voice softens. "They're so pretty. Thank you."

"Nah, they've got nothing on you." His tone is almost reverent and his piercing gaze holds mine.

"Don't forget to find us later, lovers," Candace says.

Neither of us look away as she leads her friends away. I swallow, willing my confused heart to calm down.

"You still came," I say.

Alex furrows his brows. "Why wouldn't I? You came to my game to support me, of course I'm here for you. I said I wanted to take you." He gives me another appreciative once over, licking his lips. He touches the gauzy ruffle in my tiered gown and rubs it between his fingers. "Wow. You really do look amazing."

Our deal is over, I remind myself. "You look really nice, too."

His shoulders relax. I realize how stiffly he was holding himself.

"When you didn't answer my calls or texts last night or today, I was worried. I'm guessing you heard what Mike said when you left the room. I'm sorry."

I slide my lips together and find an empty table near the back to set the flowers on. He follows me.

"You're all I've thought about. I've been calling and texting. I got up early to come see you, but you were already gone. I've been running all over trying to find you today. Then I ditched practice. Coach Lombard will probably burst a blood vessel next time he sees me. Or my knee caps." He rubs the bridge of his nose, averting his eyes. "I would've been distracted the whole time if I went and probably would've walked out."

I twist my fingers together, surprised to hear he'd put in so much effort. I haven't looked at his messages, too afraid of what they might say.

His gaze snaps back to mine and he steps into me, cupping the side of my neck. The uncertainty shrouding my heart battles with the need to lean into the touch.

"The whole time I wanted to be right here with you, sweetheart. Are you okay?"

The question throws me off. I don't want to admit I spent a long time crying over him last night because there's nothing between us except the agreement we made. It makes my chest constrict when he scans my face and runs his fingers over me as if there are physical wounds he can mend for me.

"Yes?"

"Yes?" he echoes in the same doubtful tone. "Shit. I knew I should have gone after you last night. After I punched out Mike, you were gone. Theo said I should let you cool off."

I blink in shock. "You punched him?"

He pulls a face like that's a given. "Of course I decked him. He ran his mouth about my girl. I wasn't going to stand by and let anyone say that shit about you without catching my fist for it. The guys had to pull me off."

I exhale unevenly, wishing this could be real.

"Alex, you've been kind to me." I can't look him in the eye. It takes everything to get the words out while my heart clenches. "It's okay. Mike is... Well, he's an asshole who can't handle rejection. Other than him, people haven't bothered me at all. We can finish this now. You don't have to keep pretending you're my boyfriend."

"Good."

Oh. I try to swallow, but my throat is clogged. I hug myself. Cracks splinter through my heart, then it shatters all over again.

EIGHTEEN
ALEX

LAINEY'S EYES SHUTTER. She regards me warily the same as she did two weeks ago. I want to wipe that expression away. I'll protect her from everything if she'll let me.

"Look at me," I urge. "I realized something last week. Do you like me?"

"What? I thought we were only pretending," she says in a small voice that makes me want to wrap her in my arms and never let go. "Until you kissed me for real. But I've heard about your reputation, I thought—"

"No. That's not why I kissed you." I blow out a breath. I have to tell her this to make her understand what I'm trying to say. "At first, yeah. I just thought if word got around I was your boyfriend, people would leave you alone. I never made time for girlfriends because hockey is the majority of my life. I had no idea it was like this. I mean, I felt like I'd lost it because all I could think about was you."

Her lips part as I grab my chest. I'm not done.

"I like you. In case you didn't notice, I'm kind of obsessed with you." I release another unsteady exhale. "Do you remember when I spent a week at your place before summer training camp?"

"Yeah."

"I got up in the middle of the night for a drink and you were in the kitchen. You had a book under your arm and an old Flyers hoodie on." Her cheeks turn pink. I hold her shoulders. "I really wanted to kiss you then."

Lainey's eyes widen. "You did?"

"Hell yeah. God, you looked hot in nothing but that hoodie."

"I didn't know you were watching." She ducks her head, then hesitates before resting her hands on my chest. "Why would you like someone like me?"

"I like you because we fit. Just like this."

Dropping a hand to grasp her waist, I tug her against me. She emits a cute little noise of surprise. I brush my knuckles along her cheek.

"We might seem like opposites, but it's what makes

us click together like puzzle pieces. I like that you get excited about your books and how hard you work. When you're shy and stick close to my side, I like being the guy who gets to be your buffer between you and the world. It makes me feel good to protect you." I take her chin between my fingers and hover my mouth over hers. "And I really like the way you sound screaming my name when you come for me. That's when you know how to be loud. Just for me."

Air rushes past her lips and her lashes flutter. She sways against me.

"Alex," she whispers thickly.

"Yeah, sweetheart?"

"I like you."

"*Good*," I say with the same conviction as earlier. "Because I want to be your boyfriend. No more pretending."

Lainey gets what I mean this time. She grabs me by the lapels and pulls me down for a kiss. I smile into it, locking my arms around her. I could kiss her all night.

Her laugh breaks us apart. She hides her face against my chest.

I squeeze her nape, enjoying the easy access with her hair braided in a crown. "What is it?"

She shakes her head. I press my lips to the top of her

head, finally taking in the room. The decorations are great and people are enjoying themselves.

"You're amazing," I murmur. "Look at this place."

The praise gets her to peek up from my chest. "It came out better than I hoped."

"You worked your ass off for this. Let's go enjoy it." Tipping my head to the dance floor, I lift my brows in question. "Dance with me?"

She blinks. "You know how to dance?"

An amused huff leaves me. "Don't underestimate all the ways coach likes to make us train. We do all kinds of stuff to hone our coordination."

Lainey slips her hand in mine and I lead her to the dance floor, giving her a twirl through the fog hovering above the floor. My girl looks stunning, the layers of her black gown fanning out. Tugging her back to me, I tuck her against me and rest my hand at the small of her back.

A warm ember burns bright within me, encasing my heart in light whenever she smiles. After dancing, we do the photo booth. She picks out a crown made of crystals. I lift her in my arms like a princess, enjoying the way she clings to me.

When the night winds down, I trace her spine and bring my mouth to her ear. "Want to sneak away?"

"I was going to help the volunteers that are cleaning up," she says.

"Let them handle it." She shivers when I kiss the spot below her ear. "I want to hear you say my name. Actually, I want to hear you scream it knowing you're mine."

She smothers a gasp. "Alex."

"That's a start." My teeth graze her neck and my mouth curves at the tiny sound that escapes her. "We could hit up the library."

"Oh my god. No." She swats at me, then takes my hand to pull me toward the table with her flowers on our way out.

My chuckle echoes in the hall outside the room, the music muffled the further we move away from the dance. It's a shorter walk to the hockey house from this side of campus, but I don't want to bring her there for this. I want her all to myself with no chance of interruptions.

On the way to her dorm, I shrug out of my suit jacket and drape it over her bare shoulders. She flashes me a grateful smile that I have to kiss. She giggles when I do.

When we make it to her dorm I sit on the bed, watching her set her flowers on the desk before slipping off her shoes and gloves.

"Come here." I pat my thigh. "Let me help you out of your dress."

Lainey stops just out of my reach. She bites her lip. "What is it?"

She sighs. "When we've fooled around before, I— You really want this?"

I shoot to my feet and snag her hand. "Yes. Fuck, you have no idea how much I want you." I run my fingers through my hair. "I've only ever had sex without strings. I've never been so consumed by a girl until you. I've been trying to go slow with you because I wanted it to mean something more when we did this."

The trepidation clears from her face and she lifts her small hand to cup my jaw. "Fresh start?"

"Yeah." The corner of my mouth lifts. "I'm claiming more of your firsts tonight. They're all going to be mine, baby."

Her eyes gleam. "You can have all of my firsts."

I capture her mouth in a kiss that starts slow, then heats up fast. Fumbling for the zipper on her dress without breaking away, I manage to drag it down while she loosens my tie and unbuttons my shirt. She presses her body against mine and with a rough noise, I lift her by her waist and lower her to the bed.

Ditching my shoes and pants, I crawl over her until I'm settled between her luscious thighs. I watch her face when I grind my cock against her, only the thin barriers of our underwear separating us.

Lainey tips her head back with a gasp. "Oh."

"Like that?"

She hums, giving me a little nod. "More."

"I'll give you everything you want, baby."

Kissing a trail down her throat, I peel the cups of her bra down, closing my lips around a nipple. The noise she makes is my new favorite. I rock my hips into her while my tongue teases her tits. Her nails dig into my shoulders and she moves with me until she freezes.

"You come for me, sweetheart?" I rasp against her flushed skin, giving her other nipple the same treatment. "You get off with just my cock rubbing against your clit?"

Lainey wraps her legs around my hips. "Yes. I want to feel you for real."

I lean up to kiss her, then get up to find a condom in my pants and strip off my briefs. When I turn around, I find her naked and waiting on the bed.

"Fuck, you're beautiful."

The flush I love so much spreads across her chest. I finish putting the condom on and stroke a wisp of hair that came loose from her braid off her face.

Once I'm in position between her legs, I thread our fingers and pin her hand to the bed beside her head. She looks so fucking gorgeous spread out for me.

"Hold on for me. Don't let go."

"Okay."

I go slow, captivated by the look on her face while my cock sinks inside her pussy inch by inch. She's hot and *tight*—fuck, her body grips me like a vice. It's tighter than when I had my fingers stuffed in her last night, her body stretching to fit my length.

Her chest heaves and a wrinkle appears on her forehead. I want to smooth it away.

"You doing okay?"

"You're just—big," she pushes out with another gasp. "I feel so full."

My head hangs and I restrain myself before I ram inside her. "Shit, babe. Don't tell me that right now, or I'm going to come. You feel so good."

I kiss her to distract myself from the heat shooting through my dick. When she gives me permission to move with a nod, I groan against her swollen mouth.

Keeping a slow pace, I drag my cock out, then make her take every inch again. She bites her lip and arches for me. I bury my face into her neck, finding all her sensitive spots while I fuck her with steady, sharp thrusts that make her breath hitch.

"That's it, sweetheart. You take my cock so well," I rumble.

She moans, thighs squeezing my sides. "Alex."

The next snap of my hips hits her harder, my cock throbbing. "Again."

"Alex," she cries louder.

"Yes, baby. Scream my name." Reaching between us, I stroke her clit. "Tell the world you're mine."

When she does, I bite out a curse and bury my cock in her pussy as my orgasm spirals through me. I keep moving my hips and petting her clit until she shudders again, then pull out and collapse next to her in the tiny bed.

I prop my head on my palm and trace her heart-shaped lips. She smiles, kissing my fingertips. Flashing me a devious glance, she flicks her tongue out to taste them.

"Careful, or I'm going to keep going until you're wrecked."

Her lashes flutter and her brown eyes flare with desire. "Did you borrow that line from the book?"

I smirk. "Maybe." I tug on her lower lip with my thumb, then tuck the loose strands of her hair behind her ear. "Are you okay?"

"More than," she says.

I give her a soft kiss before getting up to take care of the condom. When I return to the bed, I pull her against me and spend a long time kissing her until she's breathless. My cock twitches against my thigh, but I'm not in a rush. Drowsiness claims her first, her head resting on my shoulder when she dozes off.

Laying with Lainey in my arms, I make a change to the future I've been chasing. When I make it to the NHL, I know my girl will be with me.

NINETEEN
ALEX

A group of us walk from our place to get coffee in town. It's been a few days since the dance and today's the first afternoon we haven't had our schedules get in the way of spending time together. When we said we were leaving, half the house decided to join us.

Her fingers are laced with mine as the rookies lead the way, Theo and Higgins bringing up the rear.

"You know, you guys could've gone for coffee later," I point out.

This was supposed to be a date and they're all crashing it.

"Nah," Theo counters, doing a shit job at covering his amusement. "You seemed like you wanted extra company. The more the merrier."

"I'm going to kill him," I mutter.

"It's fine." Lainey squeezes my hand. "I still get to see you."

She told me about the emotional and cathartic conversation she had with her dad the night before the dance after she left the party. I encouraged her to talk to her brother, too. They had a family dinner last night at their dad's place so she could work through her feelings with them. I wanted to go with her if she needed me, but she insisted it was long overdue and something she should do on her own.

Things are back to being good between them today. Better than it was before. They seem closer after talking it out.

"Do you think they still have donuts today?" Easton wonders aloud while rubbing his stomach. "I could crush some donuts."

"If you eat that you'll have to put in double the work in the gym," Higgins reasons in his gruff, quiet way. "A donut sounds really good, though."

Lainey laughs. "I want a fresh, warm muffin."

My teammates groan. Most of us keep to a strict diet during the season. She catches on, ticking treats off on her fingers.

"And maybe a chocolate filled croissant. Banana bread. Those macadamia nut cookies they always have are magic. Oh, and the danishes."

The guys make noises of despair. Each option she suggests makes my mouth water. It's nothing compared to how much I crave her.

"Okay, now you're just torturing us, babe." I pull her into me and lock my arm around her waist. "You're a little menace."

She beams and I have to kiss her.

"Enough of that." Theo bumps into us without much force to break us apart. We reach the coffee shop and he holds the door open. "Come on, get inside. It's cold."

The place isn't as packed as usual. Cameron and Easton find an open spot for all of us to sit.

"What do you want?" I ask Lainey. "My treat."

She clutches her wallet. "I was going to treat you."

I chuckle and grasp her waist, stepping into her. "Nah. I beat you to it."

"Is this really how it's gonna be all the time?" Theo eyes both of us. "Because I'm going to need to invest in, like, ear plugs or something."

Lainey grins. "You'll just have to get over it."

Once we have our order, we sink into the comfortable seats near the stone fireplace crackling with a warm fire. Lainey sets her muffin down on the low table and Easton stares at it with so much longing she laughs.

"Do you want some?" She holds the plate out to him.

He shakes his head. "I really shouldn't. I already cheated by eating so many pizza rolls Friday night."

Cameron pats his shoulder in solidarity. "Think of what coach would say."

"Here. This really isn't going to kill you. At most, you're looking at an extra jog around the block to burn it off." She breaks off a tiny piece. "I'll be sworn to secrecy."

Easton makes a whole show of savoring his little piece. Theo rolls his eyes and Cameron snorts at his exaggerated moans every time he eats a crumb.

Shaking my head at his ridiculousness, I shoot a smirk at Lainey. She leans against my side, right where she belongs.

Cameron and Easton wrestle with each other on the way out of the coffee shop once we're finished. Higgins follows behind with his hands in his pockets. They stop messing with each other when two girls wave at them from across the square, diverting to meet them while Higgins continues toward the house.

Theo hangs back. "Where are you going now?"

"I want to go to the bookstore," Lainey says. "You boys can come if you want."

Theo holds up his hands. "No thanks. You're going

to look at your porn books. I don't want anything to do with that."

"They're not like that." His eyes snap to me in surprise. "What? I've read one. It was good."

"It's not about the sex." Lainey lifts her chin. "It's about love. You'd learn a lot if you read a romance book."

"I'm not looking for love." He backs away. "Later."

She snickers when he leaves. "I was hoping none of them would want to come."

"Oh, so now you want me alone?" I tease.

"All to myself," she agrees. "Just you and me between the bookshelves."

I slide an arm around her waist and guide her in the opposite direction. "Like our own mini library."

She elbows me. "We're never doing anything there besides studying."

My grin stretches. "I bet I can change your mind about it, sweetheart."

The store is fairly busy when we go inside. Business has been booming every time I pass this place.

With a secretive smile, Lainey leads me to the romance section where things are a little quieter. "Since you liked the cowboy one, I have another book I think you might like."

"You know what I like?" I nudge her until her back

hits the shelves, then brace my hands on either side of her and dip my head.

"What?"

"You."

My mouth presses against hers and she holds on to my sides.

"Excuse me," a woman says.

Lainey breaks the kiss, cheeks pink. A customer motions to the section we're blocking.

"Sorry." She blushes and pushes me until I fall back a step. "Oh, if you're looking for the next generation series of those books, we have that in stock, too. It's really good, I've read it."

The woman smiles. "Thank you."

She makes a quick selection and leaves us alone in the aisle.

I step behind Lainey, bringing my mouth to her ear. "Pick out what you want me to read next and any other books you want."

She spins to face me. "Don't say that if you don't mean it."

The corners of my mouth lift. "Good thing I mean it."

She points out a series featuring a team of hockey players and leaves me alone. A laugh catches in my throat when she finally returns a while later with a huge stack.

"I really had to narrow it down," she laments. "These are my top choices."

I take her books to carry them for her. "You could've gotten them, too."

Her eyes widen. "Seriously, you can't say that to a book lover. You're toying with my emotions." Studying the stack, she tilts her head thoughtfully. "I think I can pick three from this, but I'm still trying to figure out which series I want to start."

Holding back a grin, I make my way to the line. When I set the entire stack on the counter, she doesn't realize I'm buying them all until I'm paying.

She gasps. "Wait—Alex. I said I was picking three."

"I want to get them all for you." I shoot her a wink. "We'll come back for the other ones you wanted later."

She's speechless, her cute mouth parting. I gather our purchases and guide her out of the bookstore. We've walked almost a block before she finds her voice again.

"You're crazy for that. Thank you for buying me books."

"I want to give you everything."

Books. Happiness. My heart.

Her frazzled expression softens with affection. "Thank you."

"Come on. If we keep an eye out, we'll be able to sneak upstairs without anyone noticing so they leave us alone."

I set the new books down on my nightstand when we get back and pull her into my embrace. Her chin lifts and I meet her lips in a searing kiss I've been craving all afternoon.

We tumble to the bed without stopping, getting lost in each other for a long time.

"Hey, sweetheart?" I finally murmur against her mouth.

"Yes?" she answers breathlessly.

"That wasn't a pretend kiss."

"I know."

She releases a happy little hum, resting her forehead against my chest. I like when I've got her tucked against me like this. It makes me feel like she's protected wrapped in my arms.

"Good, good. And this?"

I roll her to her back. My lips trail down her neck, pausing to kiss her soft skin because I love the way it makes her shiver. I hold her closer, sliding a hand up to cup her nape while I lavish her throat with another reverent kiss.

"Yes?" She tangles her fingers in my hair, angling her head to give me better access.

"Not pretend." Kiss. "Not fake." Kiss. "Not an act."

"Alex," she pleads.

"Hold on, baby. We have to make this clear. I don't want you doubting that this is how I feel about you. Never again."

I plan to take every opportunity to make sure she knows I'm hers as much as she's mine. I won't be the reason for her tears again.

My only goals now are to be the reason Lainey Boucher smiles every day and to become her favorite hockey player.

TWENTY
LAINEY

April, Two Months Later

THE TIME on the clock runs down and I clutch Candace's hand, yelling my support for Alex as he and Theo fly down the ice. The puck passes between them on a breakaway that could mean victory for Heston if they make this. Each defensive player they evade has us screaming louder.

"Go, go, go!" Candace shrieks. "Oh my god, yes!"

Her enthusiasm is infectious, helping my introverted tendencies adjust to a level I'm comfortable with when I have her as my emotional support extrovert. More importantly, my boyfriend's about to score and make it to the Frozen Four for the second year in a row.

He's hoping for an NHL draft pick later this summer and I want to see his dreams come true.

Theo passes to Alex with lightning moves. I hold my breath as Alex prepares to shoot. I've seen them line up shots like this countless times in the last two months for every game I attended.

Alex slaps the puck and it sails into the net, missing the opposing goalie's outstretched glove by mere inches. The packed arena goes crazy when he scores the goal. The final whistle signals that Heston wins.

Candace hugs me with a squeal. "They did it!"

I return the hug, willing my pounding heart to slow down. The players spill onto the ice, celebrating and taking a victory lap. Alex skates right for us, lifting his helmet off. I meet him at the boards wearing his alternate jersey.

Sweaty and red-faced, he gives me that broad grin that makes my heart swell. He kisses his glove and presses it to the glass. I don't hesitate before touching my hand to meet it on the other side.

"Your goal was amazing," I say. "I'm so proud of you."

It amazes me how quickly things change. Two months ago I came to my first game in years, hating everything about hockey. Now I'm dating one of Heston's best players in recent history and my appreciation for the game has been revived. My life changed forever at my Ballgowns for Books benefit when Alex stopped pretending and became my real boyfriend.

It turns out, happily ever after isn't only in the books I read. Now I enjoy them together with him.

Theo skates by and hooks an arm around Alex's shoulders. I give my brother a thumbs up. He smirks and responds with a smug nod. They push away from the boards to head for the locker room.

Candace takes charge to lead us through the crowd. We make our way out of the arena to meet them at The Landmark to celebrate their win once they finish cleaning up in the locker room.

It doesn't take them long to burst through the doors at my dad's sports bar with their teammates a short time later. The whole place is full of people congratulating them. Alex stops a few times to shake hands and take photos with his fans. I watch from the table tucked in the corner.

This spot is my favorite in the bar because of the great vantage point while being out of the way when things get rowdy.

It's also where the photo of me and Alex dancing together at my ball hangs on the wall, along with a copy of my donation to the bookshop after the event.

After we talked, Dad takes every opportunity to tell

anyone who will listen how proud he is of me and my achievements. He's only beat out by Theo singing my praises whenever I'm spending time hanging out with the hockey team. I feel like I'm part of their weird little family.

I'm not in my brother's shadow anymore. I never was.

There's no one who bothers me anymore, either. Mike was the worst offender and he's no longer a problem. Not long after that party, he lost his eligibility to play football because of academic probation. He transferred to a community college. I never did get to tell him off, but his old group of friends steers clear of us.

Heston University is still my picturesque academic haven, and now I enjoy it more than ever, even when everyone obsesses over our hockey team.

Alex weaves through the bar to reach me at our table. He drapes his arm along the back of the booth and tilts my chin up to capture my lips. When he breaks away, he lingers there for a moment.

"Hi," I say against his mouth.

"Hey, sweetheart."

"Great game." Candace holds her hand up for a high-five.

"Thanks." Alex claps his palm against hers.

Theo and a couple of the other guys join us. One of

the freshman players winks at Candace and she laughs at his flirtatious antics.

"Did you order food? I'm starving." Theo pats his stomach.

"Wings, wings, and more wings," I say. "Like, the whole menu."

Theo and Alex both groan appreciatively. After letting hockey and its players back into my thawed heart, I've learned to order twice as much food as I think we'll eat. Proving me right, the guys descend on the food as soon as our order arrives.

Rather than feeling left out, I'm comfortable to sit and enjoy the company. They all talk and I don't feel like I need to jump in to be seen. Alex rubs my back and steals wings from my brother's plate to put on mine until I'm stuffed.

When we've eaten our weight in wings and seen every local station's sport segment coverage on tonight's game, I squeeze Alex's wrist beneath the table.

"Ready to go?" I ask.

He pretends to think about it. "You know I could talk about hockey all night."

"Maybe I'll pick my book boyfriend over you tonight," I sass.

Chuckling, he presses his lips to my ear with words meant only for me. "Or I could read it to you and become any fictional man that tries to steal your heart from me."

Heat spreads through my cheeks. I like it when we do that. "That sounds good, too."

He cradles my cheek, sinking his fingers in my hair. The affectionate moment isn't for show. I learned how tactile he is after we started dating for real.

I lean into the touch and he tugs me closer, murmuring in my ear again. "No matter what, you're my girl, sweetheart."

EPILOGUE
LAINEY

August, One Year Later

ALEX HOLDS my hand as he hauls his last bag out to his truck parked in front of my house. He spent the end of summer break with us.

While I'm getting ready for the fall semester, he's on his way to the start of his future in Elmont, New York to play for the Islanders.

He was their draft pick last summer in the first round. Rather than wait for him to finish out his time at college, they offered him a contract this year for the upcoming hockey season.

As proud as I am because he's worked hard for this, my heart gives a faint twinge of loneliness. I've prepared myself all summer for this. Not only for the distance this will put between us physically, but the possibility that with that distance he'll realize what we have isn't so special after all. He might be the one who suggested all the ways we'll stay in touch, but the reality is he probably won't have the time or energy he plans to put into our long distance relationship.

Frowning, I push the pessimistic thoughts from my mind.

This is his moment and I won't ruin it with my old insecurities flaring up.

They're born from a combination of my mom's affair splitting my family apart and my own isolation habits. It's been a long time since I've faced them after working through how I felt with my dad and Theo, and learning to come out of my shell. I have no reason to doubt my boyfriend.

Alex flashes me a sidelong look. He's been the quiet one all day and it's throwing me off. Maybe he's nervous.

"I'll text you when I get there. At least I'm only a few hours away. We won't be far from each other."

I duck my head with a soft smile. He's always able to tell when I'm down without me needing to voice it.

"Hockey players are on the road a lot," I say. "You'll be adjusting to a new team and training schedule at the professional level. You should focus on getting to know them. Don't worry about me."

He pulls a face and my smile stretches wider while he tosses a duffel bag in the truck. "But we're home during the break after midterms. You'll come down then, yeah?"

I slip my arms around his waist from behind and hug him tight to hold me over until I see him again. "Of course. I'll miss you, but I promise I'll be okay."

Tension bleeds from his body and he turns around. "Good."

Alex captures my waist between his large hands and guides me to lean against the truck before rummaging through his bags. "I got you something."

I accept the book-shaped package and smirk. "You're the one we're supposed to be celebrating."

He doesn't respond, watching me carefully. Almost nervously.

Beneath the wrapping, I find the book I've been reading. The familiar bookmark sticking out gives it away. He took it off the pile on my nightstand.

I shoot him an amused look. "Thanks, babe. You're so sweet and thoughtful." I stretch on my toes to kiss his cheek. "Great taste."

"Open it," he urges.

Examining the book, I find there's something inside where my place is marked creating a slight disruption. I open it, then blink at what's inside.

Shock filters through my system. There's a simple handwritten note beside my bookmark.

Will you marry me? (Not pretend ♥*)*

The words barely register because the ring tucked between the pages slides down, in danger of falling. I catch it, setting the book behind me on his truck bed.

Not pretend has become my two favorite words in Alex's vocabulary. He's always reminding me after a kiss or when he tells me he loves me that this is real for him.

The engagement ring is simple, yet beautiful. It perfectly suits my style and I immediately fall in love with its understated elegance.

"Alex," I whisper.

He cradles my hand the same way he's done hundreds of times, brushing his thumb over my knuckles. It always calms me down and grounds me.

"I told you once that I'm a man who goes after what he wants." He gives me that lopsided smile I love. "I know exactly what I want, sweetheart. You. Forever."

My eyes widen. "You're serious?"

A warm laugh leaves him. "Yes, baby. I'm always serious when it comes to you. Do I have to remind you again with another not-pretending kiss?"

"You're crazy," I mumble.

He grazes my forehead with his lips. "Crazy about you." Leaning back, his eyes meet mine. "I didn't want to make this big change and have you thinking you were left behind because I signed an NHL contract. I wasn't going without making sure you knew that first. It doesn't matter where I go, which team I play for. My heart is yours, Lainey. So will you marry me or not?"

My heart squeezes. "Are you sure? We're so young."

"We can wait as long as you want to make it official," he says quickly. "I just want everyone to know you're mine. To know someday I'll get to call you my wife."

I draw in a sharp breath, biting my lip. He gazes at me earnestly, green eyes full of love.

"That would make you my husband." A laugh bubbles out of me as it sinks in that we haven't been temporary for a long time. The lonely doubts clinging to me evaporate. "I like the sound of that."

He nods, squeezing my waist. "Me too, baby. If you say yes, we can go to the courthouse right now. Or we can wait. It's up to you. I'm all fucking in."

I laugh again, leaning my forehead against his chest.

Somehow I manage to nod, realizing a moment later I'm saying yes over and over.

Alex crushes me in a hug, an exhale huffing out of him that's half a relieved laugh, half a groan. "I thought you were going to leave me hanging. Holy shit. You said yes." Another laugh leaves him. "We're getting married."

"You're going to make me drop the ring." I can't stop grinning, clutching the engagement ring so it doesn't slip from my grasp while he holds me in his strong embrace.

"Let me."

Grabbing my waist, he boosts me to sit on the truck bed and takes the ring from me. I hold out my hand and he slides it on my finger. I admire it as warmth spreads through me.

"I love it," I murmur.

Alex rests his forehead against mine. "Marrying you is better than any goal I've ever scored or will score."

* * *

Need more swoon-worthy Heston U Hotshots?

Read ICED OUT, Easton's college sports romance with his rival's sister and meet more irresistible Heston U hockey players and their feisty matches off the ice.

ABOUT THE AUTHOR
STAY UP ALL NIGHT FALLING IN LOVE

Veronica Eden is a USA Today & international bestselling author of addictive romances that keep you up all night falling in love with spitfire heroines and irresistible heroes.

She loves exploring complicated feelings, magical worlds, epic adventures, and the bond of characters that embrace *us against the world*. She has always been drawn to gruff bad boys, swoony *sin*namon rolls with devastating smirks, clever villains, and the twisty-turns of a morally gray character. When not writing, she can be found soaking up sunshine at the beach, snuggling in a pile with her untamed pack of animals (her husband, dog and cats), and surrounding herself with as many plants as she can get her hands on.

* * *

CONTACT + FOLLOW

Email: veronicaedenauthor@gmail.com

Website: http://veronicaedenauthor.com

FB Reader Group: bit.ly/veronicafbgroup

Amazon: amazon.com/author/veronicaeden

facebook.com/veronicaedenauthor

instagram.com/veronicaedenauthor

pinterest.com/veronicaedenauthor

bookbub.com/profile/veronica-eden

goodreads.com/veronicaedenauthor

ALSO BY VERONICA EDEN

Sign up for the mailing list to get first access and ARC opportunities! **Follow Veronica on BookBub** for new release alerts!

New Adult & Contemporary Romance

Made in the USA
Middletown, DE
16 October 2023

40922708R00132